# Sawman Werebcar

(Saw Bears, Book 4)

T. S. JOYCE

# Sawman Werebear

ISBN-13: 978-1537787152
ISBN-10: 1537787152
Copyright © 2015, T. S. Joyce
First electronic publication: April 2015

T. S. Joyce
www.tsjoyce.com

All Rights Are Reserved. No part of this book may be used or reproduced in any manner whatsoever without written permission, except in the case of brief quotations embodied in critical articles and reviews. The unauthorized reproduction or distribution of this copyrighted work is illegal. No part of this book may be scanned, uploaded or distributed via the Internet or any other means, electronic or print, without the author's permission.

NOTE FROM THE AUTHOR:
This book is a work of fiction. The names, characters, places, and incidents are products of the writer's imagination or have been used fictitiously and are not to be construed as real. Any resemblance to persons, living or dead, actual events, locale or organizations is entirely coincidental. The author does not have any control over and does not assume any responsibility for third-party websites or their content.

Published in the United States of America

First digital publication: April 2015
First print publication: September 2016

Editing: Corinne DeMaagd

# ONE

Brighton Beck scanned the hole-in-the-wall diner his alpha, Tagan, had ordered him to meet at today. A cloud of smoke plumed from the kitchen as the cook worked furiously on the lunch rush orders. The tables were all full except for a couple of booths off in the corner and a single table in the center.

Brighton picked the table right in the middle so Tagan couldn't bawl him out. If he did, at all. His alpha was much better than the last one. He was wary around humans and didn't like to draw attention to private Ashe Crew affairs.

He should probably just man up and take the

verbal lickin' in the corner booth, but he still didn't have control over his animal, and he couldn't let Tagan see how bad off he was. No need for the crew to worry about him. It wasn't like they could do anything to fix him, anyway. No one could.

The bell dinged over the front door, and Brighton stopped shredding the napkin on the table in front of him. Tagan's nostrils flared, and he frowned at a mousy-looking woman at a two-top table near the front, then swung his bright blue gaze to Brighton.

With a nod in greeting, he made his way to the counter and ordered a hamburger and sweet potato fries to go. Even over the noise of the murmured conversation around him, Brighton could make out his request from all the way across the room. He was more in tune to the Ashe Crew. Humans were easy to ignore.

"You look like shit," Tagan said as he took the seat across from him.

Brighton snorted and leaned forward on his elbows, waiting.

Tagan cocked his head and stared at him for a long time, then mirrored his posture, leaning toward him. "You know why I called you here?"

To yell at him and order him to come home. Brighton shook his head instead of answering. That was the upside to having no voice. No lies, no shaky words, no way for other shifters to tell when he wasn't telling the truth.

"You've been gone for three months now. You haven't been returning Denison's texts, and he's worried about you. Hell, I didn't even know if you'd show up today. I know the battle at the landing was hard on you. I know seeing that asshole who tortured you was…" Tagan leaned back and ran his hands through his hair, then sighed. "I can't pretend to understand what that was like, but at some point, we need you back. Logging season is coming up quick, we're down a man on the jobsite, Haydan is shite on the processor, Denison isn't singing at night anymore without you, and if I'm being honest, the trailer park ain't the same without you in it. It's just not."

Brighton felt someone watching him and slid his gaze to the woman at the two-seater table. She had medium brown hair, pulled back into a ponytail, not a stitch of make-up on, and her eyes looked hollow, as if she were sick. She wore a sundress of thin, dark material printed with tiny flowers, and clunky black boots with the laces untied. Cornflower blue irises watched him intently, like she could hear every word Tagan said. But she couldn't because she smelled human, which meant she had dulled senses just like the rest of her kind. Humans were practically deaf.

When he looked at Tagan again, his alpha was staring at him with raised eyebrows, waiting.

Brighton scribbled onto a small notepad he kept in his back pocket. *I'm not ready to come home yet.*

Tagan crossed his arms and relaxed into his seat. "Brooke's pregnant."

Brighton jerked his head up and stared at his alpha in disbelief. Already? But it took shifters years to get pregnant. That's what he'd been told his entire life, and now Tagan's mate was going to have a cub? A smile took his face, the first in months, and the stretch of his lips felt good. The Ashe Crew was going to have a cub. He leaned back and looped his fingers behind his head.

Whatever Tagan saw on his face pleased him because the alpha laughed and shook his head. "You should see the shock on your face right now."

Oh, he didn't doubt it. Tagan could've knocked

him over with a blade of wheat right now and he'd go right over. Holy shit. A cub.

"That's not all. Danielle has chosen not to Turn. Denison is going to propose to her instead. We're planning the wedding." The smile slipped from Tagan's lips. "You need to be there for your brother. He's having a hard time, too. I think he's getting some of those memories from the lab back, but he's not talking about it to anyone. Apparently stubborn runs in your family."

Hell, if Denison was getting those memories back, that was a shame. He was the lucky one, having repressed what had happened during the experiments. Denison deserved to be happy with his mate after what they'd gone through. Danielle was good for him—always had been.

*When?* he scribbled across the second line of the ruled notepad.

"A week from today."

*I'll be there.* Of course he would be there. It was Denison, his twin. He'd die for him, and he'd die for Danielle, too. They were the best part of his life.

The cashier called out Tagan's name, and he stood, then clapped Brighton on the shoulder. "It's good to see you, man. We've missed you."

Emotion thickened in Brighton's throat as he watched Tagan grab the to-go bag of food and saunter out of the restaurant.

Brighton went back to shredding the napkin as he thought about all that had happened at the trailer park since he'd been on his bender. No, not him. His friggin' bear. His inner monster had more control than he could ever let the others know, and until he found some kind of compromise with the snarling animal inside of him, going back to the Ashe Crew was off the table.

"Can I eat beside you?" a timid voice asked.

Brighton jerked his attention to the unassuming woman who was now standing beside his table, holding a basket with a half-eaten hamburger in it.

He scented the air again, but she still smelled like a human, and right now, he trusted them about as much as he'd trust a rattlesnake. He shook his head and watched her face fall.

She made to go, but stopped. "If you don't talk any, I don't mind. I don't talk much either."

He gave her a hard glare and gritted his teeth. Times like these made him wish he still had a voice just so he could tell her to piss off and bother someone else.

"It's just," she said, voice dipping to a whisper, "I feel better around you."

Brighton narrowed his eyes. What a strange thing to say to someone she didn't know from Adam. He could see she was sick from the way her bones stuck out and the way the dress she wore swallowed her up. She looked like she hadn't slept in days, and deep, dark circles marred what would've been a pretty face. Whatever was wrong with her, he couldn't help her. He couldn't even help himself right now.

Brighton shook his head again in denial, and her shoulders slumped.

"Thanks anyway," she murmured, then made her way back to her table, clutching the plastic red basket with her lunch in it.

He needed to leave, but something about that girl made him sit glued to his chair. There was something peculiar about her. Not her, but in the air around her. He could sense tiny vibrations drifting from her skin, but she didn't look uncomfortable or overly stressed. Just sad.

But the more he stared, the harder the air that hovered just above her shook. And suddenly, she looked up at him, wide-eyed, then went rigid and collapsed onto the floor.

He was to her in moments, but hell if he knew what to do. Her hands were clenched, her neck arched back, and her face was a mask of fear as her body seized. She couldn't go on like this forever, could she?

"Oh my God, what's happening to her?" asked a man poised above him who smelled rank with the scent of grilled onions. "Someone call 911!"

The woman's eyes were closed tightly now as her body convulsed. Panicked, Brighton lifted her head off the tile floor and yanked his belt off in one smooth motion, then shoved the leather between her teeth. Seconds dragged on as he covered her with his body, stroking her hair out of her face and wishing he had a voice to murmur nonsensical words to her.

Her body drew in on itself, relaxing from the seizure, and she gasped. As Brighton leaned over her, cradling her head, she opened her eyes, and he froze. They churned silver, like mercury, and now he smelled it. Fur.

He didn't know how she was doing it, but she'd been repressing an animal inside, and now her inner beast was clawing to get out of her.

This woman wasn't human at all.

She was a damned grizzly in disguise.

# TWO

Brighton didn't think, only reacted. He pulled the limp woman against his chest and bullied his way out the door.

"Hey!" a woman with worried eyes called as he passed. "I'm calling an ambulance. I don't think you should move her! Where are you taking her?"

Brighton ignored her. She wouldn't ever know it, but Brighton was saving the woman's life. He was probably saving everyone in the joint, because if the woman in his arms shifted here, her inner animal was going to be pissed and out for blood.

Repressing her grizzly. Brighton almost snorted.

How stupid could she be? That was like poking an alligator with a two inch stick. Once her bear got her way and ripped out of her, there was going to be hell to pay. His bear was scary enough, but damn, a pissed off she-bear was a terrifying sight to behold.

He kicked open the door with his heavy work boot and strode straight for his car. He shot a worried glance down at her, but she remained placid in his arms, staring up at him with tired, sad, silver eyes, as if she couldn't remember how to move. Or maybe she didn't want to. She reeked of bear. *Hang on, girl.*

His beat-up clunker Chevy pickup was parked around the corner in the parking lot of Sammy's Bar. His heart pounded as he turned the corner and nearly ran into a lady holding a little boy's hand. She shrieked and yanked her kid out of the way as Brighton lurched around her.

The woman in his arms slid her arms up his chest and around his neck before she squeezed her eyes closed and pressed her face against his sternum. He stared down at her as she cuddled up to him like he was some fuzzy teddy bear and not a damned monster. She'd managed to shock him to his middle. Who was this woman?

As if she'd heard his thoughts, she whispered, "My name's Everly Moore. If I don't make it, tell Momma I'm sorry."

When she let off a little helpless, pained sound, he had to close his eyes momentarily and steady his breathing before he shifted right along with her. She needed to stop. Stop being needy and hurt and sad.

A deep humming came from within him, the closest to a growl he could manage and, shit, she was drawing his bear from him. What was he supposed to do with her? He couldn't just leave her here to let the world know bear shifters existed. He of all people knew how dangerous it was for humans to know about them. But sticking her in the front seat of his truck within touching distance...well, that seemed even more dangerous somehow.

He didn't have a choice, though. The woman had to come with him. He'd have to find out who her people were and take her back there, dump her on them, and be done with her. Yep, that was exactly what he was going to do. Then he could go back to trying to sort out his own life instead of meddling in someone else's.

With the fingers he had hooked under the back

of her knees, he yanked the handle to his truck and settled her as gently as he could into the passenger's seat, then buckled her up, ignoring the small crowd who had gathered at the mouth of the parking lot. Apparently, the onlookers had followed him from the diner. Freakin' great.

He slammed the door too hard, but it was out of his control now. His bear was clawing to get out of his skin, his eyes probably blazing bright silver. Slipping on a pair of sunglasses that he had hooked on the collar of his T-shirt, his hands tingled like they always did right before an involuntary Change. His truck was about to be shredded by not one, but two grizzlies, and damn it all if this wasn't the worst idea he'd ever had.

He slid in behind the wheel, cranked the engine, then peeled out of the lot, fishtailing and spewing gravel behind him. He sped through a stale yellow light and hit the back roads out of Saratoga.

A low snarl came from the woman, but when he looked over at her, she had her eyes closed and looked white as a phantom, as if she'd passed out cold. He sped down the old logging roads that led to his cabin nestled in the Wyoming wilderness. But with every mile that passed under the tread of his tires, the humming in his body grew harder to manage. He was shaking now, hands gripped on the steering wheel, trying to anchor himself to his human skin, but he was losing ground by inches.

Lightheaded, dizzy, cold sweats, hot flashes, no air in the cab of the truck, and rolling the window down only made his bear want out that much more. Brighton wasn't going to make it to the cabin.

Slamming on the brakes, he gritted his teeth and hunched in on himself, doubling over at the pain in his stomach. He threw the car into park, opened the door, and fell out. Mindlessly, he pulled at his shirt as it constricted around his torso, suffocating him. His insides were shredding, ripping apart as he fought the animal inside of him.

Fighting never worked.

It only made the agony worse.

Brighton threw his head back, and for the millionth time, he wished he still had his voice so he could roar his rage at the world as he Turned.

****

The sun shone right against Everly's eyelids, waking her from what felt like a sleep as deep as a canyon. Her body didn't want to work yet, but she could at least flutter her eyes open. She squinted as her vision adjusted to the late afternoon sunlight streaming through the canopy of pine trees above.

Where was she?

Grunting, she sat up, but was hindered by a seatbelt. She had fallen asleep on the bench seat of that quiet stranger's truck. She blinked rapidly and looked around. The door to the truck was ajar, and the stranger was nowhere to be seen.

"Hello?" she called, fear and confusion swirling in her chest, making it even harder to move. She always felt like grit after a seizure. Mortified, she remembered the stranger putting his belt in her mouth. He'd looked so worried, emerald green eyes wide, dark hair mussed and hanging over his forehead as he stared down at her.

She was the worst at first impressions.

And now… She searched the evergreen woods that surrounded the dirt road where the truck sat at an angle. The stranger seemed to have ditched her in the middle of nowhere.

Her luck just kept getting better and better.

Movement to her right drew her attention, and

she sighed in relief. The man was walking through the trees, straight for the truck, his eyes on her window as if he could see right through the dark tint to her.

He wore low slung jeans with holes worn into the knees over thick-soled work boots, a double cord of leather looped around his neck and nothing more. A dark beard covered the bottom half of his face, making it impossible to see his lips. He moved like some graceful panther through the woods, never stumbling or missing a step, but with his eyes on the truck, as if he'd walked that path a hundred times before. His stony chest and eight-pack abs flexed with every step, and as he swung his muscular arms, she could see the curl of inky lettering on the inside of his bicep. From here, it looked like the words read, *Always remember.* His skin was smooth and tanned over his shoulders, but perfect lines of red, angry scars ran from the defined shadowy line between his abs around his ribcage. There had to be ten at least that she could see, and all spaced perfectly, as if he'd mutilated himself for the sake of art. A chill rippled up her spine as he approached, looking tiger-striped and dangerous. His eyes stayed on her as he walked around the front of the truck.

"What happened to your stomach?" she asked through the open driver's door, unable to help herself.

He gave her a withering look, then faced his scars away, picked up his discarded gray T-shirt on the ground, and pulled it over his torso in one smooth motion.

He slid into the truck and slammed the door. Staring ahead, he clenched and unclenched his hands, looking at them as if he'd never seen them before. With a sigh, he glared at her, then slid closer. Without warning, he pressed her forward and unzipped her dress in the back.

She gasped and jerked away, but he'd already pulled it to the side, exposing her shame.

Everly froze as the man stared at the bite mark on her shoulder blade with something akin to fury in his expression.

She tried to cover it up as tears stung her eyes. The plan had been to hide that mistake until the day she died, but now this man had witnessed her seizure and her scar. She was pretty sure today couldn't get any worse.

He zipped her dress up slowly, then leaned over her lap and opened the glove compartment. A trio of yellow notepads sat in there with a new box of pens. He pulled out what he wanted and slammed the glove box closed. The sound of a pen scratching on paper filled the pickup.

*Who claimed you?* he wrote.

She shook her head and frowned, baffled. "What does that mean?"

With an impatient sigh, he scribbled, *Who bit you?*

That little gem she was taking to her grave. There was only so much mortification she could handle in one day, so she shook her head defiantly. "That's none of your business."

A muscle twitched under the man's eye. *Gray Back or Boarlander?*

Everly rubbed her face, then clenched her fists in her lap. "I don't know what that question means. Look, thank you for helping me in the restaurant, but I think I need to go home. I don't feel very well." And it was clear as a creek she'd gotten herself trapped in the cab of a truck with a nut job.

But when the man turned on his ride and

straightened it out, he didn't head back for town. Instead, he headed farther into the mountains and past logging signs that warned tourists away. And now, she was getting really nervous she'd found herself in a spot she didn't need to be in with a man she didn't really know. Again.

"What's your name?" she asked, hoping to start a conversation that would remind him she was a person so he wouldn't serial-kill her.

He didn't answer, of course. Instead, he turned on a classic rock station and didn't look over at her once. And when he pulled under a sign that read *Boarland Mobile Park*, he didn't offer any explanation.

She turned, utterly baffled on why he'd brought her to a trailer park in the middle of the wilderness. "What are we doing here?"

The man gave her a narrow-eyed, impatient look and stopped his truck in front of the first trailer. He got out and flung the door closed.

"Seriously! Why did you bring me here?" she called.

He scribbled something onto the yellow notepad and slammed it against the window.

In dark, angry pen strokes, he'd written, *I'm*

*taking you home.*

# THREE

Brighton couldn't remember being this pissed off at anyone, other than that fuckwad, Reynolds. Even Denison didn't get under his skin like this, and he was his pain-in-the-ass twin brother. No, Everly Moore definitely took the prize for riling him up.

All she had to do was answer his question about who'd claimed her. She'd guarded her answer like some damned dragon protecting treasure. What did he care who'd bit her? He just needed to know who to take her back to and who needed a verbal beat down for allowing a dangerous shifter in town—unescorted. Whoever her maker was had put

Brighton and all of his people in danger by allowing her out into the world with no control over her animal.

He stormed the tiny trailer with the office sign hanging lopsided over the mold-riddled door. Harrison was alpha here, and if Brighton was lucky, he'd have an answer on where he needed to dump Everly. As far as alphas went, Harrison wasn't bad. Hell, he'd had a drink with him on a couple of occasions with Denison and Tagan. He was really hoping Everly belonged here with the Boarlanders and not with the Gray Backs. Those idiots were less savory in general.

He banged on the door, then stood back. And when no one immediately answered, he banged again. Boarlanders trickled from their trailers, one by one, and silently watched him glare daggers at the alpha's house.

Rustling sounded from inside, and Brighton crossed his arms over his chest and leaned back against the porch railing.

Harrison opened the door, squinting into the sunlight like he'd been sleeping. "Brighton? What are you doing here, man?"

Brighton jerked his chin toward the truck where Everly was staring at them with her mouth hanging open.

"Who's she?" Harrison asked, rubbing his dark eyes sleepily, then running his fingers through his sandy-blond hair in a half-assed attempt to straighten it.

Brighton scribbled across the pad of paper, *Please tell me she's one of your claims.*

Harrison read the note, and his eyebrows shot up. "She's a bear?" He looked back at the tiny woman in the truck and shook his head. "She ain't one of ours. My boys aren't ready for mates. None of their bears are interested right now, and I laid down orders last year to run potential claims by me first."

Dread thumped painfully in Brighton's chest. That was bad news. *Can you make sure?*

"Boys," Harrison called to the seven shifters gathering around the porch. "Answer me one at a time. Did you claim that girl?"

A short, stout man in his mid-thirties shook his head and answered, "No."

A tall, muscled, Viking-looking shifter followed immediately. "No."

Five more negative answers and not a single false note in any of their voices. Shee-yit. If she was a Gray Back, no wonder she was fucked up.

*Thanks*, Brighton wrote, then nodded respectfully to the alpha before stepping down the porch stairs.

"Hey, Brighton?" Harrison called after him.

Brighton paused and turned, waited.

"Look, I've talked to Creed, and he said his crew is doing the same thing as mine. Their bears aren't looking for mates, except for one. Matt Barns. You know him?"

Brighton nodded and hoped to God Everly wasn't Matt's claim. He had been a powerful ally to have in the battle at the landing a few months back, but the cagey shifter wasn't overly nice to women. Brighton and Denison had pounded his face up a few times at Sammy's bar for pushing women too far, too fast. If Everly was his, no wonder she hadn't wanted to tell Brighton who made her.

"Look, you want my advice?" Harrison asked. "If you ain't a hundred percent sure she's Matt's mate, I wouldn't go parading her in front of the Gray Backs. You don't want them knowing there is an available female bear in the territory, if you catch my drift."

Oh, Brighton caught that drift just fine. She'd have every bear in that Gray Back camp vying for a skinny dip in her pants. They'd be relentless. A lady bear was able to handle rougher bedroom antics than a fragile human.

He nodded his head in silent thanks, then strode back to the truck.

The Boarlanders were a hardworking cutter crew who chopped down the lumber on the new job sites the Ashe Crew was ordered to clear. They were nice guys for the most part, though extremely competitive. Perhaps Brighton had made a misstep coming in, guns blazing, ready to dump Everly onto them. Already, the Viking shifter had taken a couple of steps toward the truck as Brighton reversed. Even if their bears weren't ready to settle down and commit to a mate, that didn't mean they didn't like sex.

"Why are they looking at me like that?" Everly's voice trembled from the passenger's seat.

Her hands were clenched in her lap, and the bitter scent of fear wafted from her skin. It tore at him, so he rested his hand over the thin fabric of her dress and squeezed her thigh. Heat flooded into his fingertips, and he yanked his hand away. Everly gasped, as if she'd felt it, too.

Brighton looked down at his hand, half-expecting it to be red where his fingers had touched her. When nothing was amiss, he turned the truck around and headed back down the single lane dirt road, determined not to look at her again until he figured out what to do next.

Whoever Everly Moore was, she was affecting his snarling bear like a drug.

And for the life of him, Brighton couldn't figure out if that was a good thing or a very, very bad thing.

\*\*\*\*

Everly was terrified. Those men back there had shifted their attention to her immediately, and their eyes—they weren't right. They looked hungry in ways that made her skin crawl.

Back on the main road, the man, Brighton, the blond-haired guy at the trailer park had called him, pulled the truck to the side of the road. He breathed deeply, shoulders lifting, and stared out the front window as the steering wheel made a pathetic creaking sound under his choke-hold grip.

When he looked back at her, his eyes looked different, too. Lighter than before, but perhaps it was a trick of the saturated afternoon sunlight bouncing off the hood of his truck and against his face.

He mouthed something and gestured to her shoulder blade, but she didn't catch it. She hadn't been paying enough attention to his lips with his eyes holding her frozen.

*I need to know who bit you*, he mouthed again.

Heat flooded her cheeks, and she sank back against the cool window. Slowly, she shook her head. "I can't."

*Can you tell me who didn't bite you?*

"What do you mean?"

*Was it Matt Barns?*

"I've never heard of him."

Brighton waited with his dark eyebrows arched high.

"No. It wasn't him. Why is the stupid mark so important to you?" Because it was sure as sugar flakes mortifying to her, and she definitely didn't want to keep talking about it every five minutes.

Brighton's shoulders fell, and he leaned his head back against the seat, chin up as he narrowed his eyes and stared above the truck at the branches that bent and swayed under the will of the wind.

He rolled his head toward her again, and this time he didn't look so severe. Instead, his eyes had cooled, and he looked resigned. Slowly, he mouthed, *Where do you live?*

"Twelve twenty-three Rochester Avenue, apartment B. Back down in Saratoga." For now. The eviction notice her landlord had left on her front door this morning was about to ruin her life even more than it already was.

Brighton nodded and turned the music back up, apparently dismissing any further discussion, and proceeded to ignore her the entire way down the winding mountain roads and switchbacks, all the way to the curb in front of her apartment building.

"Great," she said, feeling awkward. "Well, it was nice to meet you, I think." She hesitated at the strange sensation of saying goodbye to someone who had made her feel steady for the first time in months, then slid from the truck and made her way toward her front door, pulling her keys from her satchel as she went.

The engine cut off, and the sound of a slamming

door and crunching boot steps in the gravel behind her was loud against her new, and annoying, sensitive ears. Six months of hearing every little cricket chirp and cat meow two blocks over. If the seizures didn't drive her to insanity, her forever tingling eardrums would.

She turned her suspicious gaze on Brighton as he followed her to the front door. "No need to walk me. I'm perfectly safe now."

He muscled past her, plucking the keys from her grip, then unlocked the door to apartment B and barged into her house. What in the hell did he think he was doing?

She followed him in as red anger blasted through her veins. "Brighton!"

He turned and canted his head as a curious smile took his lips. She was stunned into silence at how that little smirk transformed his face. Without the anger, he was quite handsome. His nostrils flared, and he made his way down the hallway and to her bedroom.

"Look, I think you got the wrong idea," she said, following directly. "I'm not inviting you to sleep with me. Not that you aren't an attractive man and all with your brooding silence and nice arms...and your pecs and incredibly defined abs. But beards aren't my thing."

Brighton spun in the door frame of her room, humor quirking his lips. He stroked his beard thoughtfully as his gaze dipped to her lips. Then he turned and headed straight for her dresser. And when he reached that, he yanked open the top drawer and began pulling out her panties—her panties!— as if they were BFFs.

"What are you doing?" she screeched, shoving them back in the drawer.

Irritatingly, he pulled them back out again and stacked them on her bed.

Shocked and embarrassed, she sat on them to hide the mortifying mixture of cotton hipsters and lacy see-throughs. Hooking his hands on his hips, he frowned at her as she sat on the pile as if she was trying to hatch an egg.

*Fine,* he mouthed. *Then you do it.*

"Do what?"

*Pack.*

"Pack for where?"

*You can't stay here.* His lips formed the words slowly, deliberately. *Not like this and not alone. You'll come home with me.*

"Come home with you," she repeated. He'd lost his damned mind. Or perhaps he didn't have it to begin with. "I'm absolutely not coming home with you. You just took me into the wilderness and paraded me in front of a bunch of hungry-looking mountain men who probably haven't seen a girl in years, and now you want me to come home with you? That isn't what normal people say yes to Brighton."

Brighton made a single click sound behind his teeth, then pulled a notebook and pen from his back pocket. *You wanted to eat by me today. Why?*

"It wasn't to sleep with you or chase some common-law marriage with you or anything like that, if that's what you think."

Brighton silently scoffed. *I have no interest in any kind of marriage to you. I'm offering to help you. I don't want you at my house any more than you want to be there.*

"Then why are you asking me?" Her voice was pitching higher, but damn it all, he was pissing her off. Not only that, but now he was making her feel completely undesirable with his smirk that said he didn't even find her remotely attractive. She'd already had her fill of low self-esteem, thanks to the last man she gave that kind of power to.

Crimson was creeping up Brighton's neck as he glared her down. He shook his head as his pen scratched away at the paper, stabbing holes in a couple of places. *You can't stay here. Not like you are. It isn't safe for you or anyone else.*

She clenched her fists and stifled a shriek that was clawing its way up the back of her throat.

The anger fell from Brighton's face as his eyes roved over her arms and neck. He shook his head and made a calming gesture with his hands, palms facing her. *No, no, no*, he mouthed, but she wouldn't be settled down now. He was being ridiculous and pig-headed and—

Queasiness stabbed through her middle a split second before her body froze up on her. Helplessly, she dropped to the floor. She stared at the white ceiling fan, spinning lazily above where she had left it on all day. The sea foam green walls closed in on her by inches as her stomach lurched like she was falling from the top of a roller coaster. And just as her head was about to hit the Berber carpet, he was there. Brighton. Just like he had been before, with the same worried moue to his lips. With the same concerned frown as he cradled her head against his thighs. His muscles were tense and made a terrible pillow, but right now, all she knew was pain. Lightning bolts zinged up her spine, but she was unable to arch her back to relieve the burning sensation. She couldn't draw breath, and her teeth clamped down until her jaw felt like red, hot agony.

She was going to suffocate. She was going to die right here in Brighton's arms.

Her lungs burned for oxygen as the outer edges of her vision collapsed inward, growing dimmer until all she could see were Brighton's eyes. They were the color of melted metal, churning like ocean waves as he gritted his teeth and searched her face. Hallucinations. Another symptom to add to the list.

But even with those demon eyes, he looked like he cared, and if she had to go, at least she wasn't alone. At least she was with someone who would feel sad after she was gone.

# FOUR

The smell of fresh, homemade rolls and butter woke Everly up. Her Sunday school teacher had once told her there was no hunger in heaven, so Everly knew she hadn't keeled over just yet. When she opened her eyes, the first thing she saw was exposed rafter beams above her. She was in a small cabin and stretched across the only couch in the living room. A stone fireplace nestled crackling flames, which seemed to be the only light in the place besides a lantern that sat on a small dining room table. It illuminated a plate of steaming food.

She sat up and pushed the green and blue plaid

blanket Brighton must've covered her with off her lap. Movement in the shadows by the fireplace drew her gaze. Brighton stood from a crouching position. She could only make out his outline and his eyes, which were reflecting strangely in the soft glow from the hearth. Silently, he approached, then offered an oversize, calloused hand.

It felt dangerous to touch him with his eyes all bright like that. He kicked up something about her instincts she'd never felt before. Safe one moment, at risk the next. He waited, staring steadily at her, so she had no choice but to touch him. She slid her palm against his. Tendrils of numbing warmth traveled from her fingertips to her wrist, settling whatever hunch had told her to be wary.

He pulled her up surprisingly easily, as if her weight was no more than air. Then he placed his hand on her lower back and guided her to the kitchen table. She thought he would sit and eat with her, but instead, he backed away and leaned his hips against the woodgrain countertop in his small kitchen. He crossed an arm over his middle and bit his thumbnail as she placed a napkin in her lap.

"Did you cook all this?" she asked, staring at the

steak, cubed potatoes, mixed vegetables, and a smaller plate with two rolls, sopping with melted butter.

He nodded once.

"Well, color me impressed."

Shoving off the counter, he reached for a cabinet and pulled out a glass. When it was full of water, he set it in front of her and pulled the notepad out of his back pocket.

*You're too skinny.*

She frowned in disapproval. "Rude."

He sat in the chair next to her and scribbled away. *Something is wrong with you, but you don't smell sick.*

"Also rude to comment on people's smells. And I know something is wrong with me. I lost my dad-gummed job waiting tables because of the stupid seizures. And now they come faster and faster, but when I took the medicine my doctor gave me, it only made me sicker."

Brighton shook his head, then wrote something on the next line of the ruled paper. For emphasis, he jammed his finger at what he wrote. *You can't take medicine. Of course you got sicker. Didn't anyone explain this to you?*

She had the uncomfortable feeling that whatever he was talking about was circling slowly back to who bit her, so she shoveled a forkful of buttery, cubed potatoes into her maw to avoid any more conversation, and oh good Lord! That was the best thing that had ever touched her tongue.

"Aw, hell, Brighton. You should be on one of those chef shows on television." She tasted the mixed vegetables, which seemed to have been sautéed in some kind of sauce made of unicorn smiles and baby giggles. The steak was cooked at a perfect medium, and when she bit into the warm roll, she was second guessing her assumption that she hadn't died and gone straight up into the clouds.

When she looked up to compliment him again, his lips were quirked in a smile. Brighton was quite fetching when he looked happy. The scowl had gone, and in its place, his deep green eyes danced as he watched her eat. His nose was straight, eyebrows dark and animated. His teeth were straight and white.

"I bet you look all right under that beard," she said before she thought about her words.

The smile dropped from his lips, and he canted

his head, as if he couldn't figure her out.

"I mean, that is to say, you probably look like one of those magazine ads. You know, the ones with the underwear models with the pretty faces. Not that you're pretty. You're a burly, manly man if ever I've seen one. Beefy, too. And not that I'm imagining you in your underwear..." Her gaze dropped to the taut muscles in his neck and the perfect line between his pecs that she could see between the two undone buttons on the green thermal shirt he'd changed into. She cleared her throat and forced her attention back to her food. "I'll shut up now." That lasted about a second before she felt compelled to explain. "Sometimes I ramble when I'm talking to people who don't really want to talk back to me. Like my momma. Not that you don't want to talk. I'm sure you'd want to if you could." She scrunched her nose apologetically. "Balls. I'm sorry. I shouldn't talk about you not being able to talk. Is it a choice? Are you doing it for artistic reasons? Or were you born this way with no voice? I read about religious members who choose not to talk for a year, sometimes more. You aren't one of those fellows, are you?"

Brighton blinked once, slowly, and when he

opened his eyes again, they looked dead and cold. She could see him shutting down on her, slamming down walls to protect whatever secrets he obviously didn't feel like sharing with a stranger.

"Right. I probably shouldn't have asked you that either. It's none of my business."

Uncomfortable, she slowly sawed her steak into bite-size pieces as he leaned back in his creaking chair to study her. Careful not to bring up anything else that would earn her an angry look from Brighton, she finished her meal in silence.

*You had a job?* he wrote as she chewed on her last bite of vegetables.

"Yeah." Shyness crept over her, and she lowered her gaze so she could hide the heat that was creeping into her cheekbones. "I've seen you in Boomer's Grill before. You probably didn't notice me, though. I waited on you a couple of times. You and a couple of big gruff-looking fellows."

A slight frown took Brighton's face as he leaned back in his chair again and dragged his gaze over every inch of her face. His eyes lit up, and he leaned forward and scribbled across the last line of the paper. *Your nametag said Ever. I remember you now.*

"You probably don't remember me by my face. It's okay. I'm plain Jane boring vanilla. That's what Momma always says. She says I need to grow some brains because no one's gonna kiss me on looks alone. You probably remember the strange name on my tag. Momma thought I was gonna keep her and Daddy together forever. So…" She shrugged. "Everly, and my friends call me Ever for short. Well, not really friends so much as co-workers. I'm kind of shy around new people, and old people, and then when I get nervous I just talk and talk about nothing at all, and it puts people off." She cleared her throat and gave him an apologetic smile. "So, you see, you not talking doesn't make any difference right now because apparently I'm going to talk enough for the both of us. I don't think I've strung so many words together since…" Since *him*. Everly gritted her teeth and wished she was a mute, too, right now, just to save herself the embarrassment of her flapping tongue that wouldn't shut the hell up.

*The job?* he wrote.

"Oh, yeah. I had about ten too many seizures at work, and I was scaring the customers away and spilling drinks all over everyone. I don't know what set me off. I've been having them for six months now, but before that, I never had a one in my life. Can I tell you something?"

He looked amused and nodded.

"It's really easy to talk to you."

*Because I can't talk back?*

"I guess so. But also, I don't feel as awful around you. I feel…calmer."

*You're having those seizures because you aren't letting your bear out enough.*

Everly read the words on the new piece of notepad paper three times, but they still didn't make a lick of sense. "I don't understand. Is bear short for some sort of disease?"

He drew a rough outline of a snarling bear with big teeth and claws and arched his eyebrows. Then he wrote, *I'm a grizzly, too. No use hiding what you are from me.*

"Like a grizzly bear?" A chill rippled across her forearms, and she leaned back in her chair, eyeing the distance to the door.

Brighton might be a nice person, willing to help her through a couple of seizures and feed her after, but he was also showing signs that he was about three bubbles shy of a soda. She'd already dealt with crazy before, and she sure wasn't doing a repeat of that.

*Gig's up*, he scribbled. *It's in the eyes. You can't hide what you are in the last seconds of your seizures. You need to let your animal out, or she's going to kill you.*

Kill her? Oh no, no, no. Everly was *not* stuck in the woods with a stranger in the middle of God knows where, and now he was turning out to be a serial killer? Fear clogged her throat, making it hard to draw a breath. "Thank you for the dinner, but I need to be going."

She stood and walked backward to the door, then snatched her purse that was sitting in an old wooden rocking chair beside it and held it against her chest like a shield. "It was nice to meet you." Nice and terrifying.

Brighton sat where he was, frozen as he watched her leave through narrowed eyes. With his dark lashes lowered like that, his eyes sure did look different. Feral.

Everly clutched her purse tighter and backed out the doorway, then stumbled on the trio of stairs on the other side of the porch. Catching herself on the railing, she gasped as she realized she didn't have a car or any other means of escape. And even if Brighton had left the keys in his truck, he hadn't parked it in the front yard, and she had no idea where it was. Heart pounding as she searched the empty field adjacent to the cabin for anything that would aid her, she jogged toward the dirt road that led to the woods beyond. If she could just find a main road and flag down a car, she'd be set.

A whimper wrenched from her throat as she began to sprint, her thick-soled boots clunking heavily against the gravel with each hurried step. Brighton didn't seem to be chasing her, but that didn't dissuade her rampant need to get out of here as soon as possible. She ran until her legs burned and her feet dragged the ground. She ran until she couldn't see his house down the long road when she looked back over her shoulder. Until all she could hear were the crickets and the frogs and the wind through the branches above her.

The road curved, and when she looked back one last time, all she could see was wilderness. She turned and smashed into a wall of muscle. When

Brighton gripped her arms, she screamed in terror. The man hunched in on himself, as if she'd decimated his eardrums, and damn it all, her ears were ringing, too, but it gave her a split second when his grip loosened to make a run for it.

Brighton grabbed her elbow and yanked her to face him, then reached over his head and pulled off his shirt.

"What are you doing?" she cried, flashbacks and horrid, painful memories flooding her. She couldn't survive this. Not again.

The full moonlight bathed his face in shades of blue as he slowly mouthed, *I'll pull her from you.*

"You're insane!" she said, jerking hard to escape his grasp.

His fingers were like an iron vice on her arm.

"You're hurting me."

Brighton released her immediately, eyes wide. *I'll pull her from you, and you'll feel better.*

"Stay away from me," she said as she backed away from him.

He followed slowly, kicking out of his boots.

"I said stay back!"

He unbuttoned his pants and pushed them past

his hipbones, past more stripes of scars. "Please," she pleaded in a whisper. "Don't do this."

*I won't hurt you.*

A smattering of pops echoed through the woods, like the snapping of bones, and Brighton grew larger. And as a scream lodged in her throat, an enormous beast burst from him.

Shocked into stillness by consuming fear, she gasped to release her terrified shriek, but couldn't find the voice to do so. Who would hear her, anyway? This couldn't be happening. Black, curved, dagger-like claws ripped from his fingers, and dark fur exploded from his body, covering him completely. His face morphed into something terrifying and wild as he stood to his full, towering height. Petrified, she stooped and covered her ears as moisture burned her eyes.

No, no, no. This wasn't possible. Brighton wasn't a bear. That wasn't even in the realm of possibilities. Bear men didn't exist!

As he fell forward on all fours, the earth shook with the force. Made of weapons for ripping and maiming, his paws were bigger than her head. He'd brought her all the way up here to kill and eat her.

She wasn't Brighton's friend.

She was his prey.

Horror locked her legs, and she fell backward into the dirt. She landed hard on her elbows, scraping one against a jagged stone. Pain zinged up her arm, and the scent of iron filled the air. She was sobbing now as tears streamed down her face. Brighton stood over her, one paw on either side of her shoulders, then he buried his nose against her neck.

Something was opening inside of her, hurting her, shredding her. She bowed against the pain, but it didn't help. The hurt grew from her middle, increasing in intensity until she clenched her hands and cried out. Brighton pushed a giant paw under her, scratching her back through the thin material of her dress. He pulled her against his chest, and she knew the end was coming.

Her throat slammed closed, and her body went rigid, and this time Brighton wasn't going to help her through the seizure.

He was going to kill her.

# FIVE

Brighton didn't understand. All Everly had to do was Change—give the bear her body and she wouldn't seize anymore. She wouldn't feel sick or waste away. He was calling to her bear, could sense her just under Everly's surface. Hers was a quiet bear, perhaps the most submissive he'd ever encountered, but it shouldn't hurt her like this to Turn. It shouldn't be this hard.

Unless she didn't know her bear existed yet.

Shit.

Clamping his canines against the pain of another Change so quick, he squeezed his eyes closed and melted back into his human skin. She wasn't breathing. He cupped her face and searched her wide, terror-filled, silver eyes. Her bear was right there, so why wasn't she coming out?

"Breathe," he whispered. Pushing air particles through his ruined throat felt like swallowing glass, but he wanted her to know he was right here with her.

Her body curled in on itself, then relaxed and went limp. She gasped for air, and he cradled her head, propped her up, and rocked her gently.

"I'm sorry. I'm sorry," he whispered over and over again. He deserved the pain of the soft words he forced out.

A sob wrenched from her throat, and she curled into a fetal position. She looked pale and shaken, and when he lifted her into his arms, she lay there limp. He nuzzled her forehead, unable to keep from touching her. Bear shifters needed touch and affection. Even bachelor groups hugged and clapped shoulders often. Touch was necessary to reassure himself that everything was right in his world. And right now, Everly was it. She was everything he focused on, everything he thought about. He had to fix her because no one could fix him, and it couldn't be the same for another. He had to do something good for someone who needed it because no one could ever right the wrongs done to him.

Trembling like leaves in a stiff breeze, her hands were clenched in front of her stomach.

He wanted to kiss her knuckles and make her fear go away. "It's okay," he whispered. "I won't let anything bad happen to you." Besides the bear someone had put in her.

Whoever had done this hadn't even had the decency to explain what was happening to her. Women didn't make good bears if they were too submissive. And shy, rambling Everly wasn't a personality he would've ever chosen to Turn. She was at risk of her bear pushing for control and slowly taking her mind until she was nothing but a bear in a human body. The only reason that hadn't already happened was because her bear seemed to be completely submissive. So submissive, she hadn't even made an appearance yet. Six months of seizures, which meant Everly had been bitten a half year ago. The first Change was usually instant after the bite, and here she was, still unaware of what had been done to her after all this time.

The urge to take care of her was overpowering. He'd never felt like this before about anyone, human or shifter. He cared about the women in the Ashe Crew, Brooke, Skyler, and Danielle, and would die for them if it ever came to it, but this was different. He wanted to make Everly okay again. He wanted to know everything about her. Wanted to find what made her tick, and he wanted to be the first one to meet her bear.

And dammit, he wasn't going to let her go crazy. He wasn't going to just sit by while she seized until her repressed bear killed her. He'd never be okay again if that happened. Not after the trauma that had scarred him inside and out when he was sixteen at the hands of Reynolds and his team, but maybe life would be more bearable if he saved Everly. Already, he'd gone two hours without Changing, just because his need to care for Everly was greater. Everly Moore. Ever. He did remember her from Boomer's Grill. She spoke of herself as if she was plain, but she'd been wrong. She was sick now and looked gaunt, but not even that could hide how beautiful she was. He'd watched her work at Boomer's, talking too low to customers, who in turn asked her to speak up. She'd lowered her gaze time and time again to anyone who tried to hold eye contact with her. The Ashe Crew had been talking about new machinery for their logging business up in the mountains over lunch, but Brighton had watched Everly serve tables and wondered what kind of life had made her try to be invisible like that. He liked to be invisible sometimes, too. He hadn't recognized her at the café because she looked so different now, but months ago, he'd asked to eat at Boomer's Grill the next time they were in town just so he could watch her again.

The way she looked now was her bear's fault. No, not her bear's. The blame rested solely on the asshole who put that bear inside of her, then walked away.

He could see the house now, so he cradled her closer and picked up his pace. A tear ran down the corner of Everly's eye, and he thumbed it away, hating himself for causing it.

"I'm not like that," Everly murmured. She lifted her water-rimmed eyes to his. "I'm not like you. I can't change into a bear or anything else. I'm just plain Jane. I'm just me and nothing special. Nothing scary. You have that thing tucked up inside of you, but I don't. You were wrong."

Brighton's lip twitched with how much he wished it was true that she was still human. It would've been best for her to never have been bitten at all. For her to never have met the man who did this, and for her to continue a simpler existence. But while her body had been zapped of its energy with the seizure, the bear was still in her eyes, proof of what she was now.

Brighton climbed the porch stairs and kicked open the front door, then made his way to the bathroom with her, careful to avoid hitting her legs and head on modest-size door frames. In front of the single, large mirror over the sink, he set her on her feet. She swayed, so he steadied her, searching her eyes in the last few seconds of her naivety. After tonight, she'd be altered forever. She wouldn't be able to see herself the same. Brighton was a legacy, born a shifter to shifter parents. This life was all he'd known. But Everly had been human, and she was learning here that monsters under the bed really did exist.

His chest ached as he turned her slowly toward the looking glass.

Her eyes locked on his in the reflection, then

dropped to her own. She drew in a little inhalation of breath and covered her mouth. "Oh, my God," she murmured, staring at herself.

"God didn't have anything to do with what's been done to you," he whispered, accepting the razors slicing up his throat to force the words. He didn't want to write notes anymore, or mouth words. For some reason he couldn't fathom, he wanted Everly to hear the ruined rasp that was all that remained of his voice.

Her eyes lifted to his in the mirror. "Your eyes look just like mine do." She lurched forward, as if her legs wouldn't hold her anymore.

Brighton wrapped his arms around her collar bones and held her tight against his chest. If she didn't have the strength to stand right now, that was okay. He could be strong enough for both of them. "I know you're tired and weak right now, but you need to see this and accept it so you don't convince yourself it was all a dream when you wake up and your eyes look normal again." He swallowed hard as pain seared up the back of his throat.

Everly's face fell, and her gaze dropped to the single bathroom sink. "I look terrifying."

Brighton brushed his finger under her chin, lifting her face again until she looked at herself. "Not to me. To me, you look just right."

A small, relieved smile took the corners of Everly's mouth. "I thought you couldn't talk."

Pain filled his chest at what he'd lost, at how much he wished he could talk to her like Denison talked to Danielle. His voice had sounded much like his brother's once. "It's not really talking," he whispered, then pointed to the scar on his throat, the one he could only cover up with a long beard. When he had to look at the damned thing in the mirror every morning with a clean-shaven face, his bear shredded him.

Time didn't heal all things.

Everly turned in his arms and ran her fingertip down the surgically-straight raised mark. Then her gaze dropped to his torso, striped with the scars of his youth. All in the name of science. Dark curls of anger unfurled within him as he wished she could look upon a body he didn't have to explain. He waited for the horror, the disgust on her face, but her eyes dimmed to soft blue as she drew her fingertips across each scar that curled around his ribs, one by one.

Her touch felt phenomenal against his skin, and by the time she reached the ones across his hip bone, he didn't feel so dark inside anymore or so insecure in front of her. The humming rage of his bear was being stifled like flames under a spray of water.

Between his legs, his cock swelled as she brushed his last scar, the one that curved from his inner thigh around to his ass.

Everly inhaled a long, shaky breath as she drew her attention to his erection jutting between them. "Is that because of me?"

He nodded.

Her voice dipped even quieter than his own. "That scares me."

She was telling the truth. If he hadn't heard the honest notes in her voice, he would've known from the faint bitter smell of fear that filled the space between them.

He took a step back and whipped a fuzzy white towel from the rack by the shower, then covered himself up. Only when he was sure the smell of her fear was diminishing did he lean against the wall farthest away from her and speak. "Who made you afraid of a man's body?"

She was quiet for a long time, eyes filled with sadness that gutted him. He thought she wouldn't answer, but at last she said, "The man who bit me."

Brighton slid his hands behind his back, clenching them so hard his knuckles hurt. He wanted to kill whoever had hurt Everly. She was too sweet for this world, and someone had taken advantage. Someone who was going to pay in blood by his hands someday.

"Will you tell me about him?" He had to force the words since they came out a hiss as anger constricted his throat.

"Will you tell me who did that to your body?" she countered.

He looked down at his ruined torso. One side of his profile was covered in unflawed skin, while the other was a constant reminder of what had happened nine years ago. Of course she wanted to know. Everyone who saw him without a shirt did, but he couldn't talk about it without his bear taking his body over and over and over again until he was exhausted from the pain of the constant Changes.

He tucked his chin to his chest as he leaned his shoulder blades against the wall, then gave Everly a hard look through his lashes. He shook his head slowly.

"Because it hurts to talk about?" she asked, gripping the edge of the counter behind her hips.

Slowly, he nodded.

"For me, too."

He got it. His scars were obvious, while hers were mostly on the inside. The inside scars, from his abundant experience, were much worse than the outside ones.

"I'm going to help you," he promised.

"You gonna fix me, Brighton? Because right now, it feels like I can't be fixed."

He huffed a humorless, silent laugh and rested his head on the wall behind him. He and Everly were two peas in a fucking pod.

But out of the two of them, one was going to be okay, and he was going to make sure she got to a point where she could be happy again. Where she wouldn't be sick or waiting on her next seizure, because the way her life was going right now, she wasn't living. She was just waiting to die.

Everly approached slow, then traced the scar that ran from his nipple to under his arm. "At least tell me, did someone do this to you because of the bear inside of you?"

Brighton gripped her hand and pulled her touch away from his skin, then nodded.

"Will this happen to me?" she asked.

"Never," he whispered. "The man who did this is dead."

Her eyes snapped wide. "Did you kill him?"

Brighton lowered his chin once in affirmation. She should know who he was. That was the only way trust worked. If she knew the gritty stuff and still stuck around, maybe he could trust her back. "And if anyone hurt you like this, I'd avenge you, too." And when he found out who the fuck Turned her against her will, that shithead was going to be in a world of trouble.

"So I'm a bear...person."

"A bear..." His whisper faded to nothing, and he grimaced at the blinding pain in his throat. He mouthed his answer instead. *A bear shifter.*

"Does it hurt to whisper?" she asked, concern pooling in the deep sky color of her eyes.

A nod and, *I can't do it for long.*

Her eyes dipped to where his scar was hidden in

his beard. "Why do you hide that one?"

*Because it's the one that made me the ugliest inside.* Irritation snapped through him, and he straightened his spine. *I need to take care of you.*

"What?"

*You're bleeding, and I can't just stand here chatting while you're hurt. My animal won't let me anymore.* He pulled a first aid kit out from under the sink and turned her until she was facing the mirror again.

She was a brave little thing, only wincing silently as he cleaned the half-healed scrapes on her elbow. He'd ripped her dress when he'd pulled her to him when he was a bear, and four shallow scratches were already closed up and on their way to being faint scars. Shifter healing was the best part about this gig. It was the only reason he was still alive after everything that had been done to him.

By the time he was finished, his bear was snarling to rip out of him again. It wasn't supposed to be like this, happening so quickly, but he'd been on a bender since he'd killed Reynolds, and talking about his scars with Everly had only kicked up the grit that made his inner animal uncontrollable. At least he knew he was safe around Everly when he was Turned, though. Even as unbalanced as he was right now, his animal instincts roared to keep her safe instead of grow defensive and hurt her.

His skin tingled, as it always did right before a Change. *Come on*, he mouthed, pulling her hand. He led her swiftly into the second bedroom where he'd already laid the duffle bag he'd packed for her on the twin-size bed. This had been his room when he and Denison had first rented the place years ago. He'd bought the cabin and land in secret to have an escape from the trailer park when his bear was broken like this. Now, it felt right having Everly in his bed.

His bones were splintering as he let go of her hand and backed toward the doorway. *I have to go.*

She frowned and shook her head slightly, as if she didn't understand why he had to run away from her now. "To turn into a bear again?"

*Yes.* He turned to leave.

"Brighton?"

Brighton froze in the doorframe, hands on either side, back flexed with his effort to stay human to hear what she had to say.

"I'm scared."

He looked at her, over his shoulder. "I won't ever hurt you," he rasped out.

"Not of you. Of me."

"You can't be afraid of your bear, Ever. Accept her."

"Brighton?"

A low hum emanated from his middle. He would've been growling if he had the tools to do so. He turned to look over his shoulder again.

Everly's eyebrows arched. "Shave your beard and own that scar, and I'll try to accept what I am."

Brighton narrowed his eyes at her challenge, inhaling deeply as he absorbed what she was really asking him to do—expose his ugly side. Open up avenues for her to pry into what had happened to his voice. He gritted his teeth and curled his lip for an instant before he strode from the room.

Maybe he didn't want her always looking at the scar.

Maybe he didn't want to talk about the shit he'd been through.

Maybe he didn't want anyone to actually see him, the real him.

He didn't want her to think him hideous or

damaged, even if he was. He wanted her to see him strong. If she didn't, how could she trust him to heal her?

No, she didn't need to see him weak, even if that's what he was right now.

The beard needed to stay.

It was better for both of them if his secrets remained buried.

# SIX

Everly unpacked slowly. It was clear she couldn't go back to town the way she was. If Brighton was right, and she really had a…bear…inside of her, she'd be a danger to people. When another tear slipped down her cheek, she dashed it away with the back of her hand. She was so tired of feeling weak. And it wasn't just about what she was going through now. She'd always been fragile.

In school, she'd been the quiet one. Growing up in Saratoga hadn't been easy. Momma was loud and embarrassing, and the townies all knew who she was. Sometimes Everly thought she'd been born to counteract the chaos Momma brought by being quiet and as close to being invisible as a person could become. Everly took up almost no space and had always preferred it that way, but now she was going to be a bear? Another traitorous tear slipped the inside corner of her eye, and she growled a very human sound as she wiped it away.

Turning for the mirror over the dresser, she bared her teeth like she'd seen Brighton do and said, "Grrrr." With more feeling, she tried to look ferocious and gritted out another pathetic snarl.

She wasn't bear material. In actuality, she wasn't even strong human material.

She ripped her gaze away from her gaunt, scared reflection and pulled the clothes from her eighth grade chess club duffle bag Brighton must've found in the bowels of her closet.

Okay, so she was a bear person. No, Brighton had called them bear shifters. She inhaled deeply. "I am a bear shifter."

It would be a lot easier to believe if she'd actually turned into something more than a frozen human with silver eyes. Brighton's bear was much cooler and scarier than what she'd managed thus far.

Including the time Brighton was missing from the truck, his Change in the woods, and his current status as a giant grizzly hunting for honey or fish or blackberry bushes or whatever it was that bears did in the woods, he'd shifted three times since she'd met him today. In contrast, she'd Changed exactly zero times in six months, convincing her further that there was definitely something wrong with her bear. Which wasn't surprising because Momma had always told her how abnormal she was. Hot damn, she hated when Momma and her poisonous tongue were right.

She sucked at being a human.

She sucked at being a bear.

And right about now, she felt like amoeba poop smeared on slimy moss that clung to river rocks.

Soft guitar notes sounded from outside, going louder then quieter as the wind picked them up and took them where it wanted. Her sensitive ears pricked, and she made her way around the small bed to the window. With two fingers, she drew the thin curtain away from the window.

The moon was full and high, illuminating a dilapidated barn. Clad in jeans and nothing else, Brighton sat in an old rocking chair. Blue light reflected off his shiny scars as he plucked the strings of an old, beat-up guitar. The song was a sad one, each note drawing out a lonely emotion from her and causing her to lean against the old window frame to listen.

As mortifying as it was, she'd noticed him at Boomer's, then gone stalker and went to one of his shows once. He'd played music while his brother sang, and she'd grown such a crush on Brighton. He sat outside of the spotlight, as if he didn't want to be seen, and she'd identified with that. She'd sat way in the back of Sammy's Bar so he wouldn't notice her there watching him, and she'd sworn to herself she'd work up the courage to talk to him. Someday.

And now here she was. Staying in his home in a bed that smelled like him, unpacking clothes he'd thoughtfully tucked into the duffle bag for her.

And he was a bear.

She allowed the curtain to fall and pressed her back against the wall.

Everything she'd thought she knew about the world had been dumped on its ass today. Her heart pounded against her sternum as she remembered the giant grizzly exploding out of Brighton. It looked so painful. She'd heard his bones snap, and he'd done it three times today that she knew about. Her bear was going to bring her so much pain.

She settled her clothes into an empty top drawer Brighton had thoughtfully left open, then changed into a pair of skinny jeans that tucked into her unlaced, clunky boots and an oversize teal-colored sweater that hung down to her knees. It wasn't the most flattering outfit, but the thick fabric that enveloped her was comfortable, and she felt safer all hidden inside.

Besides, it was getting colder at nights, especially in the mountains where Brighton's cabin was nestled, and she was about to go outside without a jacket. She had questions.

Brighton jerked his head in her direction as she opened the front door. In a graceful motion, he stood and set the guitar in the rocking chair behind him, then searched frantically for something.

As she approached, he stood tall and crossed his arms over his chest. It didn't cover his scars by half, and now he couldn't seem to meet her gaze.

"If you're worried about me looking at your scars, I'll try not to."

Brighton stared off into the woods, then looked back at her as his frown furrowed his dark eyebrows. His abs flexed with every breath he drew, and she made a conscious effort to keep her eyes on his.

But...his abs. And the faint trail of hair that travelled from his belly button down into his low slung jeans. And now she was gawking at those perfect strips of muscle that delved over his hip bones... "Fuck it all, Brighton. If you don't want me to stare, stop flexing, or breathing, or..." Her cheeks burned, and she looked away completely, angry that he had this much power over her. "Or put a burlap sack on, because those sexy T-shirts and thermals you've been wearing aren't going to keep me from looking at you. And if you prance around here half naked like this, I'm going to stare, and you'll just have to suck it up, buttercup, or put a damned shirt on."

Brighton looked down at his stomach, then back at her. His eyebrows lifted, and a slow, curious smile took his lips. "You aren't looking at my scars?" he whispered, and for the first time in six months, she was glad she had oversensitive ears. The better to hear him with.

"Well, yeah, I'm looking at those, too. How could

I not? They are like adornment or like a really hot tattoo. And yeah, I know it must've been agony living through them, and whoever did this deserved whatever you did to avenge yourself, but I've already memorized them, so tucking them away isn't going to matter. I have a very vivid memory. And my imagination is ridiculous. Overactive, Momma calls it."

"So you like the scars?" His frown of confusion was scrunching up his face now in an altogether adorable fashion.

"Hell yeah, I like the scars, but the muscles get me more." She poked his stomach, and it was just as hard as she imagined it would be. Her cheeks burned hotter as she glared at her finger. "I don't know why I just did that. You didn't invite me to touch you. Sooo," she said, shifting her feet. "Do you work out, or is the Adonis body part of being a bear shifter?"

His amused smile widened. "You have questions?"

She pulled the sleeves of her giant sweater down over her hands and crossed her arms over her chest. "Loads."

"Good. Sit down. You can have my chair."

"Thanks," she murmured as she sank down into the rocking chair. It creaked but was more comfortable than it looked.

Brighton disappeared into the splintered barn, then returned with a small, wooden chair.

"I'm a lumberjack. I have to stay physically fit to do my job. It's not in season right now, so my crew is all on a break, but when it starts up again, I'll be living back with them. Hopefully." He swallowed hard and grimaced.

"What does it feel like to whisper?"

"Like strep throat."

Her heart ached to see his pain, so she scooted her chair closer to his so she could see his mouth in the moonlight. "I like your voice, but enunciate, and I'll read your lips. I can't stand you hurting on my account."

He stared at her for a long time with a surprised quirk to his eyebrows. *How can you like my voice? It doesn't exist.*

"Sure it does. I hear everything now. Bear shit, remember," she said, pointing to her ear and trying not to panic at saying that out loud. She covered the frantic trembling through her middle by forcing a laugh. "What I mean is, I can hear your whisper, even if you were way over here and I was way over there." She pointed to his house. "I could tell the difference between your voice and anyone else's. It has a sexy, gritty tone to it. A good quality. I bet you had a rich, deep voice once. Am I right?"

His eyes lightened to silver, and he looked away. A muscle twitched under his eye before he swung back to her. *I don't like talking about it.*

"Okay. I'm sorry." She studied him, but he wouldn't meet her gaze anymore. Obviously, she'd made a huge misstep again. Her voice dipped embarrassingly low, but she couldn't seem to find her volume anymore. "I came to watch you play once." She scrunched up her nose and tried to find a way to make him understand her. "I don't usually talk to men except when I'm waiting tables. And the only man I ever dated...well, he turned me into this." She dared a glance at him.

Brighton lifted her feet into his lap and leaned back in his chair, shocking her to her core. *When did you come see me play?* He mouthed, fiddling with the undone lace on one of her boots.

"Last April. I sat in the back because I was too

scared to talk to you. I tried to build up the courage after your show. You and your friends did some shots up at the bar right near where I was sitting. Not your brother, though. He didn't drink anything, but you did. And you were smiling along with them, and I wished more than anything that I could be brave and just say hi. And I chickened out because that's what I do. So, you see, I don't have much experience talking to other people. And when I do, I mostly annoy them by being too quiet or yammerin' on about nothing. I'm trying not to annoy you because then I know you won't want to help me anymore. And right now, you feel like my last shot at surviving this."

*You will survive, and you'll be happy again.* His nostrils flared as he inhaled. He swallowed hard and pushed air past his ruined vocal chords. "I swear it. And you should've come and talked to me that night."

"Are your friends bear shifters, too?"

"Yeah. There are three crews of us who live around these parts. Two lumberjack crews and a cutter crew. I belong to the Ashe Crew."

"Will I have to belong to a crew, too?"

"Depends on who Turned you."

Dread slammed air out of her lungs, and she

clenched her hands in her lap. "I guess I won't belong to any crew then."

"You'll want to. Your animal will crave companionship. She'll crave comradery with her own kind. It'll take ten human friends to give you the fulfillment of one shifter in your life."

"Would you have talked to me if I approached you at Sammy's Bar last year?"

"Yes."

"Even if I was still human?"

He pulled her boot from her foot and ignored her question, which was answer enough. Brighton didn't like humans, and if she was a betting woman, she'd put down money that his animosity had something to do with the scars on his body.

He suddenly seemed very busy removing her other shoe, then her socks. She tried to draw away from him, but he gripped her ankles and steadied her. Panic flared through her limbs as he held her trapped.

"Modest?" he asked in that husky whisper of his.

"Yes."

"You'll have to get over that. If you Change while you have clothes on, you'll shred them. Stand up."

Shakily, she did so.

"You were mishandled," he whispered, leaning forward in his chair, and pushing her sweater up. "You don't have to tell me what happened for me to figure that much out. Every time I move toward you, you take a step back." He pulled the zipper of her jeans down, then stood. "I'm not him, though, and I'd never hurt you." He pulled the hem of her sweater until it was off over her head and draped on the arm of the rocking chair. "Tell me what you feel."

"I feel confused that I want you to touch me, but it gets hard to breathe, and I feel trapped."

"Tell me to stop anytime, and I will. I won't be disappointed in you." His eyes traveled to the black bra that cupped her breasts, then to the matching black panties that showed through the V of her opened jeans.

"Tell me how you feel," she murmured. "Right now. What are you thinking?"

The corner of his mouth quirked up in a pained look, and he made a single click sound behind his teeth. "Best if I don't."

"You're not playing fair."

Brighton knelt down and pulled her jeans to her

ankles, then steadied her as she stepped out of them. Slowly, his eyes looking up at hers, he leaned forward and grazed his teeth against her bare thigh, then kissed her skin, drawing up gooseflesh where his lips touched her.

"I'm going to kill the man who hurt you," he whispered, promise in his voice.

She believed him. After seeing his terrifying animal, she knew he was capable of dark deeds.

"I like the way you look," he said, drawing his hand up the back of her knee.

"Even when I'm too skinny?" she challenged him, throwing his words back at him.

He stood, then brushed his lips against her neck. "When you let your bear out, she'll let you eat again like you need to."

Her breath was coming in fast, shallow pants now as she reveled in the feel of his beard against the sensitive skin of her throat.

"Inhale deeply," he demanded. "You smell that? The bitter scent is your fear. Fear the man who claimed you has caused. The heady scent, though, that's arousal. Yours and mine."

"Yours?" she squeaked out.

He slid his fingers down to her wrist, then placed her hand against his rigid erection that pressed against the seam of his jeans.

"Whoever said you were a plain Jane is blind. You aren't plain to me. You're beautiful."

His bicep flexed as he dragged her hand up the length of him. Her breath stuttered as she imagined how much pain his thickness would cause her. Confusion swirled inside of her. Fear overpowered desire, and she took a step back, clenched her hands by her side, and hated herself for being so bad at this.

"I don't think I'm ready for this," she murmured, eyes on the ground as shame burned up her neck.

"Good," he whispered, feet planted right where they'd been.

"Good?" She looked up, the frown on her face so deep, her forehead ached.

"This will work best if you can verbalize what you do and don't want me to do. What you are and aren't ready for."

"And what is the *this* you're talking about?"

"I told you. I'm going to make you better. I think you can't shift because of several reasons, but the big one is that your bear was born during trauma. And next, I think she's submissive. Really submissive. I think you need to lighten that bag full of demons you're carrying around before she'll force her way out of you."

"That sounds painful."

He made an anguished expression as he swallowed, then forced his whisper again. "Which part? Dealing with your demons or your bear forcing her way out of you?"

"Both."

His smile was nothing shy of sympathetic. "I know you can do it."

And that right there was the most important six words she'd ever heard. She didn't know everything about Brighton, not yet. But now she knew enough. He was a good man. Trustworthy. Brighton wouldn't hurt her.

"Connor Crane bit me." It was the first time she'd uttered his name aloud since it had happened.

Brighton froze, his eyes going wide. "Connor?"

"I know you know him because he was with you that night at Sammy's Bar, and he came in with you to eat at Boomer's the second time I saw you."

Brighton backed up a step, shaking his head

slowly. "No," he whispered. Agony in his eyes, he sat heavily into his chair and looked up at her.

Get rid of her demons, Brighton had told her. Well, Connor was the biggest demon in her life. She sat on the edge of the rocking chair seat and clasped her hands in her lap. The chilly air bit into her skin, but she didn't care about that now. Red, hot fury was creeping over her just thinking about the humiliation Connor had put her through.

"Momma said my virginity was the only thing that would secure me a marriage someday, on account of my unsightly face and twig legs. She hits the bottle, and then she makes jokes about me, and it was the same a couple of days before I went to see you at Sammy's Bar. I was mad and wanted to feel wild. I stayed late that night, trying to muster up the courage to talk to you, but you left with your brother, and I felt awful. Lower than low. I hated myself for not being braver. For not telling Momma to piss off when she says awful things to me and for not going after what I wanted. I wanted you, and I let you walk right by me, within inches, and couldn't even get the word 'hello' past my lips." Everly swallowed hard and dropped her gaze to her hands. She couldn't do this if she saw Brighton looking at her like he was. Like she'd made the biggest mistake of her life. She already knew that. "He stayed behind, Connor. Bought me a drink and talked real nice to me. Even got me feeling relaxed. He seemed so nice, and he got my number before we left that night. And to my utter surprise, he called me the next day, and the next. We talked for hours on the phone, and he seemed so genuine. He acted happy to talk to me. And I had nothing to compare him to because I hadn't dated anyone before him, so I thought I'd lucked out and found a keeper. He kissed me on our second date. It was my first," Everly admitted, daring a glance up.

Brighton looked sick and had his elbows on his knees, chin resting on his clenched fists.

"I took him back to my place on our third date because it felt like the natural progression of things, and dammit, I didn't know how this all worked." Tears stung her eyes as she murmured, "He took me from behind the first time. It hurt so badly, but he said it was because I wasn't very good at it yet. I was so stupid and believed him. I thought if I was better in bed, it wouldn't hurt like that, and the next time he took me out, he seemed so angry. Like he was disappointed in how unworldly I was. That night we tried again, and I hid how bad it hurt as best I could, but he bit my shoulder at the end and I screamed. I cried and cried after he was through, but he only stood in the doorway of my bedroom with a smirk on his face. He said that now I would be a better match for his needs." She shrugged. "I was done, though. Good thing because he never called me again. And then the seizures started, and I didn't have the time or energy to think about the reasons he didn't want me anymore." She inhaled and held her breath in her lungs, then looked up at Brighton with the fervent hope that he didn't hate her now, too.

Brighton scrubbed his hands down his face and let off a shuddering breath as he linked his hands behind his head. His face was contorted with pain. He looked like she felt inside.

"Say something," she begged.

His Adam's apple dipped into the small cave at the base of his throat. His eyes were so silver, they were almost white like snow. "I did this to you. I asked the boys if we could go back to Boomer's and eat, just so I could watch you wait tables again. Connor was an asshole, and his bear was on the hunt for a mate. I hated him, and the feeling was mutual. We never got on. He saw me watching you at the café and asked me about you. I clammed up and never asked to go eat at Boomer's again because I didn't want his attention on you."

She shook her head and touched his hand. "This isn't your fault."

He stepped back, out of her reach. "Don't you see?" he asked in an agonized rasp, his eyes filling with some emotion she couldn't fathom. "Connor did this because of me. He hurt you because of me. That's just the way he was. Every seizure you've had is on me."

"Brighton, that's ridiculous."

"You don't understand. Connor claimed the woman I wanted just because he was a fucking prick with a vendetta. And now you'll pay your whole life because of my interest in you." He stood and strode off into the night. And right on the edge of the tree line, he hesitated and said over his shoulder, "I can't avenge you, Ever. Connor is cold in his grave already." Then he disappeared into the darkness.

A sob wrenched from her throat as she tried to sort through what had just happened. She'd exposed her deepest secret, the one Momma had found out and shamed her with. Now, she was a whore in Momma's eyes, giving away her virginity to a man who didn't even want her. Who didn't even call her. And on top of that, she'd caused Brighton pain just by the admission of her mistakes.

And now Connor was dead, and she didn't know how to feel.

Was she supposed to feel better when someone she'd once cared for was gone?

Relieved that she'd never see him around town again?

Glad the man who'd hurt her had received swift justice?

Right now, all she could think about was Brighton and how disappointed he'd been that she'd slept with Connor.

Her body went rigid, and this time, no one was here to cradle her head in their lap or look at her with worry in their eyes.

No one was here to care as her lungs burned and her limbs went stiff.

This time, Everly died alone.

# SEVEN

Clearly, Brighton was in over his head. He'd messed up in epic proportions last night and had come back from yet another uncontrolled Change to find Everly out cold just where he'd left her. Worse than that, she'd hit her head on the way down and split the back of her scalp wide open. Seeing her there in the dirt, alone...well, that just about caused another Change.

He had to get this shit under control. He was no good to her the way he was now.

Brighton paced the yard, clutching the note he'd written in his clenched grasp. This place had been a sanctuary—a secret hideout that none of the Ashe Crew, not even Denison, knew about. And now he was going to expose his hidey hole, and for what? A woman.

He shook his head to ward off the angry thoughts. This wasn't Everly's fault. It was Connor's fault. Brighton wished he could kill that sonofabitch all over again.

The sound of a truck picking its way up the gravel road froze him in his tracks. The urge to jog out and meet Tagan and Denison, to tell them to hurry the hell up, was overwhelming, but it clashed with his instincts to stay near Everly.

She hadn't woken up yet.

He'd spent the night thinking of how to draw her bear from her, but if she didn't wake up, he couldn't do anything.

His boots scuffed loose gravel as he began pacing again. The roiling clouds above told of an oncoming storm that fit his mood. Needing to see her face again, he rushed back inside and knelt by the bed. He'd cleaned her cut and tucked her in, but she hadn't moved in all these hours. Sure, her chest rose and fell steadily, but he'd tried to rouse her twice to no success. God, he wished he could take this burden from her. He was used to pain, but Everly wasn't strong enough for this. Not yet.

He brushed away a lock of chestnut hair that had fallen across her face. In the muted gray sunlight that drifted through the window, she had all shades of brown highlights in her hair. How had he not noticed that before? Her long, dark lashes brushed her cheeks, and a spray of faint freckles stretched across her tiny nose. Her lips were pursed, as if she were in pain, even in her sleep. And that rattle in her throat… It wasn't soft snoring—it was growling. Her bear was buried within her, but not deep enough to hide the unrest her animal was feeling.

He was safe to press his lips against her forehead here in the dim room with her sleeping soundly, so he did. He didn't regret it either. Watching over her all night had done something to him. Now, she pulled at his heart, and he hurt with worry that she wouldn't survive this after everything he'd promised.

The sound of Tagan's truck outside drew his attention to the window. He stroked her cheek with the pad of his thumb, just to reassure himself she was still warm and alive, then stood and strode out of his cabin.

"Holy shit," Denison drawled as he stepped from the passenger's side of Tagan's black Ford truck. "Now this is a trip down memory lane."

"You know this place?" Tagan asked as he exited his ride.

"Brighton and I used to live here together, back when I first met Danielle. We rented it for a couple of years right when I was getting to know you guys. Look," he said, pointing to the old tire swing attached to the giant tree in front. "I have a picture of Danielle swinging in that, and another of she and Brighton right over there in that field." He swung a troubled gaze to Brighton. "I didn't know you were still renting this place."

*I'm not*, he mouthed. *I bought it.*

His twin brother's eyes went round as dinner saucers. "You bought it? When? And why didn't you tell me?"

Brighton ran his hand through his hair and looked down at the corner of the porch. Maybe he should've told his brother about this place, but it had been nice having somewhere to hide when his bear got out of control.

"Is this where you disappear to when you leave for days on end?" Denison asked softly.

Brighton nodded once, then handed his alpha the letter he'd written. He didn't have time to get bawled out by his brother. Everly needed help, and he was desperate for any advice they could offer. He trusted Denison and Tagan more than anyone on the planet. If anyone could help him figure this out, they could. Tagan opened the folded paper and read it silently. Denison wised up and read it over his shoulder, and when they were done, they both looked at him with the most shocked expressions he'd ever seen on either of their faces.

"You gotta girl in there?" Denison asked.

"Is she your mate?" Tagan asked low.

*No*, Brighton mouthed. *I don't think so.* That didn't feel right though, denying her. He shrugged, feeling utterly helpless. *I don't know.*

"Well, that's a yes," Denison deadpanned.

Brighton narrowed his eyes and spun for the door. Bust his balls all they wanted to, but it didn't change the fact that another shifter needed their help. And not just any shifter. She'd been claimed by Connor, who had been a member of the Ashe Crew.

Everly would be a part of Tagan's crew if she survived whatever was happening to her. The quiet alpha who was following closely behind Brighton had a stake in her survival, too.

Tagan took one look at her pallid complexion and thin face and cursed.

Denison came in more slowly, nostrils flaring as he scented the air. "Her animal is barely there."

The low growling sound rumbled past Everly's lips, and she curled into herself, wrapping her arms around her waist.

"How long, Brighton?" Tagan asked.

Brighton held up six fingers.

Tagan's eyebrows nearly touched his hairline and his sky blue eyes sparked. "Six weeks?"

Brighton shook his head and jerked his thumb toward the ceiling.

"Six months?" Denison asked.

*She's Connor's claim*, Brighton wrote on his notepad. *She's never shifted.*

"That doesn't even make sense," Denison argued. "The shift takes place right away."

Brighton bit his lip as he wrote, *He Changed her without telling her anything. No warning, and just left afterward.*

Tagan rolled his head backward and closed his eyes. "Fffuck."

*Can you help her?*

Tagan read the note and shook his head. "Not if she's seizing. I'll be her alpha when she gets this under control, but I can feel her bear. Submissive as all get out. She won't trust me. Not when she's sick like this. I can try to force her out, but there's the risk that her body will seize as soon as I attempt it. And from the looks of her, she can't be doing that too many more times."

"Why would Connor do this?" Denison looked green in the face as he knelt beside the bed and studied Everly. "I thought he was after Brooke."

"Because he was a psychopath," Tagan suggested. "And likely, Brooke distracted him away from Everly, right when she needed him to tell her what was happening. Did she say why he did it?"

Brighton glared down at the notepad, sickened by what he would have to write. *Because he wanted her to be better in bed for him.*

"He hurt her?" Denison's voice wrenched up a couple notches in volume.

Brighton's shirt was constricting him, making it hard to draw a full breath. He nodded and dropped his eyes to the molding that ran along the bottom of the wall. In his middle, his insides were churning like rough seas, and his bear was pulsing against his veins, ravenous for escape just thinking about Connor hurting her.

"Brighton?" Tagan asked, warning in his voice. "Do we have a problem here?"

Shallow breaths racked Brighton's chest as he squeezed his eyes closed and tried to focus on not falling apart. Not now. He had to hold on until Denison and Tagan left.

"Stop your Change," Tagan ordered. "Now." His snarling bear settled under his alpha's demand. Slowly, his breathing returned to normal, and he cracked his eyes open.

"What the fuck, man?" Denison asked. "Should I be worried about you?"

*I'm fine*, Brighton mouthed, hands clenched.

He didn't like the way Tagan was looking at him, as if he was studying something he'd never seen before. Curling his lip, Brighton turned and left the room. And for that matter, he left the entire house. He needed fresh air to clear his head.

"Can you handle this on your own?" Tagan asked, following behind. "Brighton!" Tagan jerked his arm and spun him around. "Can you?"

Brighton leveled his alpha a look and nodded. He scribbled angry, oversize letters across an entire sheet of paper. *She's mine.*

"Nobody is disputing that. Connor has no claim on her from hell, man. What I'm asking is do you need to bring her back to the trailer park so we can all take care of her?"

Brighton's shoulders slumped, and he sat heavily on the top porch stair. Miserably, he shook his head and wrote, *I know her bear. I get glimpses of her when Everly is seizing. She won't be able to handle the crowds. Not sick. She'll never Change if I bring her to the Ashe Crew. I have to do this on my own.*

Denison pulled the notebook from his grasp and read it, his lips moving slightly as he did. "This is a lot, Brigh. If she dies—"

Brighton shot up and wrapped his fingers around Denison's throat, cutting off his sentence. *She won't*, he mouthed.

Denison pushed him off and rubbed his neck.

"Sorry," his brother said low. "I shouldn't have said that. If anyone said that about Danielle… Look, I'm sorry."

Brighton raked his hands through his hair and watched his alpha and brother get into the truck and turn slowly around in the front yard.

Denison rolled down the front window. "I know Tagan already asked you to come, but I need you there when I marry Danielle." He lifted his shoulder in a half shrug. "I need you to be my best man."

*I wouldn't miss it,* Brighton mouthed. He offered Denison the most reassuring smile he could muster, then watched them pull away until Tagan's taillights disappeared completely. A deep, aching loneliness filled him, yawning wider and wider until it threatened to swallow him up completely.

Now, he needed to Change just to forget all of these pestering, painful human emotions.

# EIGHT

"Brighton?" Everly squinted at the late afternoon sunlight that filtered through the single open window. It smelled like rain and flowers. And fur.

Pulling her nose to her shoulder and inhaling, she realized the scent of animal was coming from her. She sighed and rolled onto her back. "Why won't you come out? I can feel you right there. What are you so scared of?"

Everly knew exactly what. Connor, but how did she explain to that part of herself that Connor didn't exist in this realm anymore and would never hurt her again? She didn't understand anything about

Changing or the animal that was such a big part of her now. A sense of disconnection loomed over her, as if she didn't have the tools to reach the animal in her. Or if she had the tools at one point, Connor had snapped them all in half.

She sat up in Brighton's bed and rubbed her eyes. At least she didn't feel awful at the moment. In fact, she felt better than she had in days. The long sleep must've been good for her. When she twisted her neck, pain shot up the back of her spine, and she touched a sore spot on the back of her scalp gingerly. She didn't remember hitting her head when she'd seized last night, but she must've.

The door creaked open, and Brighton stuck his head inside. His eyes were pure silver, but relief pooled in them, making him look more human. His beard was gone, and in its place was short facial scruff that looked like it belonged on some model in a big city. Her heart thudded against her breastbone as she studied his chiseled jaws and sensual lips.

"You shaved."

Opening the door wider, he ducked under the frame and stood to his full height. He looked especially tall from her lower position on the bed, and his muscular chest pressed against the soft-looking fabric of his black T-shirt. Dark, fitted denim clung to his powerful legs, and his work boots thudded against the wood floor as he approached.

Brighton smelled of animal, too, just like her. She huffed a soft laugh and fiddled with a loose thread on the comforter before she lifted her gaze back to his. "What a pair we make," she murmured.

The mattress sank as he sat beside her. As he rested a hand on her leg, his lips curled up in a devastating smile. It was one of relief and melted her heart in an instant. She hadn't died alone after all. Brighton had found her and taken care of her. Again. Just like she knew he always would until her last breath.

His eyes didn't darken, and he clenched his jaw against some internal struggle.

"You have to Change again, don't you?"

He nodded.

"Will I have to Turn as much as you do if I get better?"

"No," he rasped out. "I'm broken. You will be perfect."

"How often for me?"

"Once every week or so, and you'll get to choose when you do it. It won't be forced."

"What's happened to make you like this?"

His eyes looked sad as he shook his head.

Hurt slashed through her at his denial. It hadn't mattered that she'd opened up to him completely last night. It hadn't mattered that she'd shared her darkest secret. He still wouldn't, or couldn't, let her in.

Stung and frustrated, she said, "I should take a shower." She stood and gathered her clothes and a bag of toiletries from her duffle bag. Without another word, she slipped into the bathroom and locked the door behind her, then hit the hot tap. When steam filled the bathroom, she stepped under the hot streams of water and scrubbed herself clean until her skin shone like an eggshell. And when the water finally ran cold, she wrapped a towel around herself, brushed her teeth, and scrubbed her face with a washrag she found in the cabinet above the toilet. Her time was limited before the next seizure would hit, and she wanted to feel clean before the next round of agony. She'd already spent way too much time rigid, on the ground, in the dirt for one day.

When she came back into the room, she assumed Brighton would be long gone, off doing bear shit. Instead, he watched her from his position on the bed, leaning back on locked elbows.

"I messed up last night. I messed everything up," he whispered.

She couldn't look at him or she'd fold and allow the water building in her eyes to fall. "It's fine. You knew Connor, so my confession must've been a blow."

"I shouldn't have left you like that."

She turned as frustration seared through her. "What could you have done? This is my life, Brighton. What Connor did cost me everything. My job. I'm about to be evicted from my apartment because I'm two months late on rent and up to my eyeballs in medical bills for something the doctors never figured out. And now I can't go five hours without seizing and having to sleep off the awful aftermath. This isn't any way to live. Good thing though, right? I guess it's preparing me, 'cause you and I both know I can't go on like this forever." Her face crumpled and she threw the clothes in her hand against the wall. "I'm scared. I'm not ready to die. I haven't kissed a nice boy or fallen in love or—"

Brighton was next to her so fast, he blurred. His lips crashed onto hers as his hand cupped her neck, dragging her closer. His lips moved against hers, rhythmically, and she gasped against his mouth. Her surprise only gave him a way to slip his tongue past her lips. The sensation and taste of him buckled her knees, and she whimpered. Kisses hadn't been like this with Connor. He hadn't cared about her. Brighton, though, was stroking the pad of his thumb against her cheek and pressing her backward until she was propped up against the wall, unable to fall to the floor in a puddle of surprise like she'd thought she was going to do.

And dammit, if this was it, if he was giving her one last good experience before she faded to oblivion, she was going to run with it.

She pushed up on her tiptoes, flung her arms around his neck, and kissed him back. He didn't smell like a man anymore. There were no traces of his cologne or the scent of his skin that was tangy with undercurrents of pine. He was raw, male animal.

"What Connor did with you," he rasped out in a barely audible whisper. "That's not how it's supposed to be. You are supposed to bed someone you care about. It'll be different with me."

"Different how?" she asked, arching her neck back as he trailed sucking kisses to her earlobe.

"I won't hurt you. I'm going to make you come instead."

Now her knees really did buckle as he rolled his hips against the thick towel she wore.

Reaching back, he stopped his affection only long enough to pull his shirt over his head. Desperate to be closer to his skin, she pulled at the fly of his jeans and pushed them down his hips until his long, thick cock was unsheathed completely.

A trill of anxiety filled her as the memory of the pain Connor had caused washed over her.

"Hey," Brighton whispered, hooking his finger under her chin and bringing her gaze back up to his. "Come back to me. I'm right here. It's just us. Just you and me."

She nodded in a jerky motion and offered him the ghost of a smile. Brighton had cared for her and never pushed her for anything she didn't want to give. He was a good man.

He twitched his head and leveled her with a

serious look. "I won't do anything you don't want me to. I promise. You want to stop now? I won't be mad or even disappointed."

She ran her finger up the length of the silken skin that stretched across his shaft, buying herself time to think. If she didn't try intimacy with Brighton, she would die with the memory of what Connor had done stamped onto her heart. And that seemed like a bigger tragedy than the bear that was slowly killing her from the inside out.

Closing her eyes, she inhaled a steadying breath and pulled the tucked end of the towel until the fabric fell in a pile around her ankles. Her cheeks heated at her boldness.

"Damn, woman," Brighton said on a breath.

When Everly dared a peek at him, his eyes still churned with the evidence of his inner monster, but he couldn't seem to drag his attention away from her breasts. They weren't anything special. Average size, she'd say, but by the way Brighton was looking at them, she'd have thought they were the sexiest things he'd ever encountered. She couldn't help the smile that cracked her face wide open.

"You're not so bad yourself there, handsome,"

she said, running her fingertips along the edge of one of his scars, the one that stretched from the crease between his abdominal muscles to his side and around to his back.

"You don't mind the way I look?"

Her heart sank at the rawness in his voice. "Of course I don't," she said, resting her palm over his heartbeat. "You're perfect to me. I wouldn't change a single thing about the way you look." She smiled mischievously. "Especially now that you shaved that scraggly beard."

His grin nearly stole her breath away, and before she could react, he picked her up, to her giggling delight, and tossed her onto the mattress, where she bounced and settled in the middle. He stalked her from the edge of the bed, his shoulder muscles flexing as he crawled toward her.

"Where do you want me to touch you?" His eyes reflected oddly in the low lighting, but his playful smile was all human.

"Here," she said, touching the faint dimple that devoted her left cheek.

He inhaled deeply, then leaned down and pecked a kiss where she had pointed.

"And here," she said, smile fading away as she pointed to the sensitive skin on the underside of her wrist.

He grazed his teeth against the pulse there, and her heart pounded harder.

"Here," she murmured, pointing to her collar bone.

Brighton settled himself on top of her, his hips cradled against hers. He pushed her knees wider with his own, then trailed kisses along her collarbone. Working his way down, the man didn't seem to need any more direction from her, and she was too breathless to give them now anyway. Brighton sure had a clever mouth and knew how to use it. He pulled one of her drawn up nipples into his mouth and kneaded the other with his hand. Over and over, his tongue lapped at her until she instinctively drew her knees even wider, inviting his cock to rest against the apex between her legs.

He bumped an extremely sensitive spot, and she rolled her hips against him to savor that feeling.

"Here," she pleaded as she pointed just under her naval.

She could feel him smile against her skin as he

moved his nibbling kisses downward. He didn't stop at her lower stomach, though. Instead, he made his way to the top of her wet seam, then spread her gently with his fingers and sucked on the spot that had her knees drawing up and her toes curling. The man was a damned magician. With a few more cleverly timed flicks of his tongue, when he covered her clit with his mouth and sucked gently again, she nearly came. And when he plunged his tongue into her for the first time, she was already done. Orgasm rocked through her body, throbbing between her legs with deep, languid pulses. But Brighton didn't stop there. Nope, he lapped at her until every aftershock had drained away.

She looked down in wonder and realized she was gripping his hair. "Sorry."

He bit the inside of her thigh playfully, then whispered, "I'd tell you if I minded. I didn't, though. I like it when you show me what you like."

"That. I liked everything you just did."

Brighton beamed at her from between her legs, like he'd just gotten straight As on his report card. "Good. Do you want to stop now?"

Everly pursed her lips and considered it.

Already, this was the most gratifying intimate experience of her entire twenty-five years. Granted, she didn't have that much to compare it to, but it sure didn't feel this good when she touched herself. There was something special about sharing this experience with Brighton. Already, her heart had tethered to him, but with every sweet, sexy touch of his fingers and lips, she felt like she was opening up. Blossoming like a spring flower. And inside, the sickness was easing. Maybe his adoration was just a beautiful distraction, but deep in her middle, she felt warmth instead of the jagged chill that had been constantly slashing her apart.

Brighton wasn't Connor. He wasn't. He could erase what that horrible man had done.

"I want more."

Brighton drew her hands from his hair and kissed her knuckles, eyes cast downward. Finally, he looked up at her and asked, "You aren't doing this just to please me, are you, Ever?"

"I like to please you," she admitted, "but that's not the reason I want to be with you. Connor scared me. I thought I would live the rest of my days terrified of attracting that kind of attention from another man." She propped herself up on her elbows and allowed him to see the honesty in her eyes. "I'm not afraid of you, Brighton. I trust you."

Adoration pooled in the deep silver of his eyes. She felt beautiful when he looked at her like this, and she smiled as he crawled over her and settled himself on top of her.

"I think I like you," he whispered as he dragged his fingers down the length of her collar bone. "You're different than anyone else I've ever met." He kissed her shoulder. "You're strong." Another kiss just below her earlobe. "And beautiful." His lips pressed against her jaw line. "You see the world differently, and it settles me. Makes me feel like someday I could look at it differently, too." A nibble to her lobe and a velvet stroke whisper against her ear. "The longer I know you, the more I think I could be good again."

Everly cupped his cheeks and searched his eyes, now a mix of silver and green. "I see you, Brighton. You *are* good."

His nostrils flared as he inhaled, as if some emotion was pushing him to calm down. Slowly, he lowered his lips to hers and pressed the head of his cock into her. A tiny gasp took her at how good he felt. Brighton had prepared her, taken it slow and easy, made her comfortable, and had worshipped her body before he pushed for this connection. It was that realization that made her remaining fear fall away. He was taking care of her, and inside, she was glowing. She angled her hips and moved with him on his next slow thrust. Gently, he slid into her, filling her. The stretch of her insides didn't hurt. It felt natural with Brighton. Perhaps because he'd been so careful to make sure she was ready and wet to take him, but more likely, it was because she was falling in love with him, and her body craved to be as close to him as possible. If she only had days left with this man, she wanted to spend them burrowed against him.

A soft moan left her lips as he eased back, then flexed his hips against her again.

Brighton's breath trembled, and his arm muscles twitched with his next stroke, as if his control was slipping. She loved it. To hide her victory smile, she kissed him, pressing her tongue gently against his. With a low hum she'd never heard him make before, he gripped her waist and rolled over, sat up until she was straddling his lap.

She giggled at how fast he was. Her stomach had dipped as if she were on a roller coaster.

"You're running the show now, darlin'. I'm yours," he whispered.

"Yeah?" she asked, rolling her hips until his eyes closed.

He nodded and wrapped his steely arms around her waist, then kissed her lips gently, plucking at them with tiny, sexy smacks until she had to concentrate to control her panting breath. As long, or short, as she lived, she'd never tire of kissing him. Of his taste and the way his lips turned soft for her. Of how eternally sexy his raspy whisper was against her ear. Scars, no voice, it didn't matter. Brighton was perfect. He was everything that was good in this world, and until right now, she hadn't known it was possible to live in a stainless moment. But Brighton made things easier, less painful. He made everything that had been blurry in her life clear as a freshwater stream. He made her want more from life.

She set the pace slow, and he allowed it. He didn't rush her or beg for her to hurry. He rasped his facial scruff against her neck in an adorable sign of affection she recognized because she had an acute instinct to do the same. His fingers gripped her back, and his powerful hips thrust forward with every stroke she allowed. Pressure built from her middle, tingling from her core through her stomach, shooting pleasure between her legs every time his thick shaft filled her. And when she couldn't stand it anymore, she bowed against him, arched her neck back, and cried out his name. He gripped her hard against him and slammed into her over and over as the first waves of orgasm crashed through her.

Her whispered name on his lips, so reverent, was the most beautiful thing she'd ever heard as his warmth filled her in pulsing jets. He eased back and looked at her with such adoration. He pushed into her again and emptied himself completely, filling her until wetness spilled out.

She snuggled against him, throbbing in rhythm to his own release, rocking gently with him while he gripped her hair and hugged her close.

"Brighton?" Happiness filled her like spring rains to an empty well.

He eased back and stroked a wayward strand of hair from her face. His eyes were the green of rain-bloated moss as he searched her face.

"I feel safe with you," she said on a breath.

A heart-stopping smile took his lips, faded as if he was unsure she was being serious, then returned even bigger. *You are*, he mouthed. *Always.*

A mixture of joy and relief flooded her, stretching from her center to her limbs, making her hands tingle like she'd been too close to a lightning strike. Chills rippled up her arms, puckering goosebumps all across her forearms as her heart yawned open. Her middle grew warmer and warmer as the first tear slipped from her eye. But as Brighton brought her palm to his lips and kissed it gently, the warmth became uncomfortable. Painful even. And with each second, the intensity grew until she was sure a seizure was coming. But as she waited for her body to freeze up and go rigid, she began to shatter from the inside out. Fire and glass and streaks of numbness shredded her until she hunched in on herself and cried out, "Something's wrong!"

And then the world went dark.

# NINE

"Brighton!" Everly's voice sounded strangled.

This was different. It wasn't like her other seizures. There was no pulsing air around her. There was no smell of sickness. Now, his senses were full of animal and fear. Gripping her shoulders, he tried to yell her name, but the word only came out as a raspy whisper.

She drew into herself in the instant it took him to realize what was happening, and with a ripping, popping sound, an enormous grizzly burst from her.

Brighton flung sideways into the wall with the force of her Change. He glanced down in shock at the painful, deep claw marks across his ribs. He could see white through the tear in his flesh. Bone. Fuck. Chest heaving, he looked up at Everly, who stood unsteady, paws splayed against the carpet of the small room as she stared at him.

He'd imagined what her bear looked like, hoped he'd be lucky enough to see her someday, but all of his dreaming hadn't even begun to touch her animal in reality. Fur as white as snow covered her body. Her nose was pink, as were the six-inch curved claws that had sprouted from her giant paws. He'd bet his ass the pads of those paws were also void of pigment, and her eyes…the silver had faded away to reveal blue as bright as a spring sky.

She was the most beautiful bear he'd ever laid eyes on.

It was in this moment, in the unusual color of her eyes, that he noticed something else. Something horrifying. She wasn't looking at him with a spark of recognition like she should've been doing. She looked terrified.

Submissive she might be, but she was cornered, and dealing with the pain of her first Change in a small room with a man she was glaring at as if he'd caused her all this grief. And an injured, cornered grizzly was the most dangerous kind of predator.

And the only escape from this room was through the door she was blocking.

"Everly," he whispered, standing slowly with his hands out in a calming gesture.

Warmth trickled down his stomach in rivers, and the room was beginning to smell of iron and his own pain. All bad news.

Her muscles tensed, and she charged. Brighton's bear ripped out of him, shredding him on the way out of his skin just as Everly tackled him. Wood splintered as his back slammed into the wall behind him. Unable to take the weight, the logs shattered and daylight hit his face as he landed on his back in the weedy side yard.

Everly was rampaging, clawing and biting as a snarl rattled her throat. He let her have him. She didn't know what she was doing, and he couldn't lift his claws against her if he tried.

He loved…

He winced as her claws raked across his shoulders.

He loved her, his Everly.

This wild, beautiful, deadly creature was it for him.

She lifted off him and spun, then barreled toward the trees. Her fur shook with every powerful lunge, and he stood, unsteady and awestruck as she disappeared into the woods. She could cover some serious ground at that speed, and she was headed in the direction of the nearest neighbor. Panic pulsed through his veins as Brighton trotted after her, then picked up his pace to a sprint as he imagined how scared she must be.

She was an easy follow. The smell of fear led him directly down her trail. Lodgepole pines and towering spruces dotted the woods, and she zigzagged through them. Pine needles prickled the tough pads of his paws, and pinecones littered the forest floor. Birds sang high in the canopy above, as if his world hadn't just been rocked by Everly's first Change.

She was slowing down. He could tell because the invisible tether that draped from his heart to hers didn't feel so tight anymore.

And when he slowed and walked cautiously into the clearing she'd chosen to stop in, he was stunned all over again. Rays of golden sunlight filtered through the thick branches above and highlighted her snowy fur. Her profile was to him, but when her eyes landed on his, they weren't vacant or wild anymore. Now, there was recognition and regret in them. Perhaps even worry. There she was.

He approached cautiously, head low, until he reached the center of the small clearing. Exhaling loudly, he sat on his haunches and waited for her to decide to bolt again or not. He hoped she wouldn't run. He wanted to touch her fur, to smell her skin and reassure her until the scent of her fear washed away completely. He wanted to familiarize himself with her animal until he'd memorized every angle.

He wanted to show her how much it didn't matter to him that she was a bear.

****

Everly's heart thrummed against her oversize sternum so fast she was afraid she'd pass out. The instinct to escape the enormous bruin that sat in the meadow before her was overwhelming. But no matter how strong her impulse, her heart wouldn't let her go. She knew him, that dark-furred grizzly nearly twice her size. *Brighton.* The word caressed her mind, flooding her with memories of him.

She crouched down until her belly brushed the pine needles that blanketed the forest floor. Legs splayed, she froze under the avalanche of fear. Terror seized her, and Brighton stood on all fours, then paced tightly back and forth, his eyes never leaving hers.

He approached a few steps, but her muscles were already bunched to flee again. She hated this! She wanted to touch him. He smelled of blood and some emotion she couldn't decipher yet.

Barrel chested and thickly muscled, Brighton's claws dug into the soft earth with every step he took toward her. His nose was black, only a shade darker than the pelt that covered his body. His fur looked soft and inviting, but still, that didn't halt the urge to run and hide from the monster grizzly bear that was inching closer.

As his shadow touched her, she flattened her ears and lowered her chin until it settled against the forest floor with the rest of her. Heart pounding, breath ragged, she waited for him to hurt her for what she'd done to him when she'd fled the cabin.

But he didn't.

Instead, he pressed his nose gently against the scruff of her neck, then inhaled deeply. And when he'd had his fill of her scent, he licked her muzzle, then rubbed his big block head down the side of her neck like an overgrown cat. A growl rattled her chest, but it wasn't a warning, like she'd given him in the cabin. This one was a sound of satisfaction. Of relief that he'd forgiven her for hurting him. And muscle by muscle, she began to relax under his careful affection. He backed up a few paces and waited for her. She didn't understand bear body language, not yet, and he was asking her something she didn't know the answer to. Slowly, she raised her head from the ground and belly crawled to him.

He snuffled against her neck, tickling her, in reward for her doing something right, so she followed at a crouch as he eased away a few more paces. More affectionate reward, and she found enough bravery to lift off the ground and press her muzzle against his.

Brighton froze and let her explore his body, the form she was still unfamiliar with. Nary a muscle twitched as he allowed her to inhale the scent of his fur. She imitated his attention and brushed the side of her face down his ribcage, and when a soft humming sound emanated from him, she turned her startled gaze on him.

He watched her, neck arched, his eyes relaxed. It filled her with warmth to know she was likely the only one who'd ever heard this sound from him.

Excitedly, she hooked a claw around his arm and tugged until he rolled onto his back, then she flopped on top of him and play bit at his neck. His chest huffed in a silent, bearish laugh. She slid over the top of him and kicked her legs out at him when she landed on her side. She wanted to wrestle, but Brighton wasn't playing back. And when the first sting of hurt feelings washed over her, he grew still, and the amused look in his eyes faded to worry. He wrapped an enormous arm around her shoulder blades, and when he pulled her against his chest, a warm, comforting tingly sensation blanketed her. He wasn't meaning to brush off her playfulness. He was being careful with her.

Burying her face against his chest, she listened to the bass drum of his heartbeat, slow and steady to match her own. She looked down at her white paws and the blade-sharp claws where her fingernails used to be. She was different, down to a cellular level, and she should be terrified of the creature she'd become. But here with Brighton, sharing the burden of being other, it was impossible to feel scared. This all felt surreal, and she had to close her eyes and inhale his scent, remind herself that this was really happening to her. As much as she hated Connor for what he'd done. Hated him for making her different and for changing her fate, he'd also put her on a collision course with Brighton. What Connor had done to her was horrific, but her experiences with that awful man had allowed her to acknowledge just how gentle and caring Brighton was. Would she have fully been able to appreciate what a wonderful man he was if she hadn't endured pain and heartbreak at Connor's hand? She didn't know. All she knew was that there was a reason she'd gone through what she had, and that reason was Brighton. She could love him with everything she had, and know she couldn't appreciate him an ounce more, because she'd seen darkness and witnessed how empty a man's heart could be.

Brighton was different.

He was everything good about what she'd endured.

He hefted himself upward, then led her out of the clearing. The trees began to feel familiar, as did the birdsong and the breeze through the branches as they walked on and on. She could settle down here and put the sickness she used to feel out of her mind. Here, in these woods, she could just be. Safety settled over her like a security blanket she'd been attached to as a child. With Brighton by her side, she didn't startle over new sounds or panic at unexpected shadows. His ears swiveled this way and that, and his eyes shifted with the movement of the forest around them, but never once did he give her any indication that anything was wrong, or that she should be wary. His easy nature out here, in his home, brought a comfort to her she never thought she'd have again.

Time lost all meaning as she adjusted to this new body. Her gait became smooth and unforced, and after a while, her ears picked up the sounds of the forest without her overthinking each distraction. She basked in the silence between her and Brighton. Here, he was just a bear. Scarred, to be sure, as his fur refused to grow where he'd been cut, but his silence mirrored her own. And when she became curious about felled logs or moss patches, he waited patiently for her to explore them thoroughly before sauntering off toward some unknown destination again.

It wasn't until she heard the running water that she figured out where he was taking her. A river snaked through the land, capped by gently rolling white-crested rapids. The water near the bank was as clear as the cloudless sky above, and she huffed in surprise as she watched tiny silver-backed minnows dashing this way and that along the shore. Everly hesitated at the edge, but not Brighton. He splashed into the water until the waves lapped at the fur on his belly.

She paced, unsure of what he wanted, then backed up a few steps and took a running leap into the river, feet landing on the stony bottom. Water splashed over Brighton, and he turned and cupped his paw, then splashed her back. His eyes smiled as she shook droplets from her fur.

Deeper he stepped until he could swim, and Everly followed, entranced by how graceful he was in the water. Brighton circled back toward her and ran his face and neck down the side of her body as she took the first two tentative strokes off the bottom.

Snorting breath, her confidence grew. She'd been

a so-so swimmer in her human life, but in this body, she was actually good at paddling around, as if her new form had been made for this place and all the many terrains the woods here possessed.

This couldn't be real. It couldn't be this easy to be a bear. This natural. She'd been human all her life with a flimsy, petit body and a bland face, but now, she was strong. Thinking of her human form made her feel funny inside—almost nauseous. And the more she thought about it, the more ill she felt, until the corners of her vision blurred. Panicked, she made her way to the bank as the pain became too much. Even the water that lapped at her skin felt like little shards of metal cutting into her. And with the sound of snapping bones echoing through the woods, she sank back into the same human skin she'd been imagining.

Stunned, she fell backward, landing hard in the shallows. She drew her shocked gaze to Brighton and watched as he melted back into a man. Where she'd felt pain, a hurt that still clung to her burning nerve endings, Brighton was smiling as soon as his face looked human again.

*Come here*, he mouthed as the waves splashed

against the strips of taut muscle that delved over his hip bones.

Still unsure of how to use her voice, she stood and wobbled over, not used to walking on two legs after walking on four.

*Take your time.*

Everly bunched her muscles and stood with her hands out, palms down to find her balance. When she was comfortable again, she made her way carefully into the water.

"I'm naked," she observed with a frown, sinking down into the water as soon as she was deep enough.

"Yeah," he whispered, reaching for her. He encircled her waist with his powerful arms and pulled her deeper until the water hit her breast line, then released her. "You'll have to take your clothes off before you Change, or you'll shred them. This is hell on a wardrobe if you aren't careful. Is your skin still sensitive? Can I touch you?"

Her skin was, in fact, tingling like a live wire, but right now, she needed him to touch her. The unexpectedness of her Change back had scared her, and her heart still hadn't stopped trying to eject itself from her chest cavity.

She stepped into his embrace and rested her cheek against his chest. From here, she had the perfect view of the claw marks—her claw marks—across his ribcage. They weren't bleeding anymore and looked half-healed already, but still, she could see pink muscle through the torn flesh.

His lips were soft against her temple. Moments turned to seconds as he let the kiss linger there, and her stomach filled with happy warmth. "I'm so proud of you," he whispered. "Ever, you did so well."

"But...I hurt you."

He shrugged and looked down at the marks as if he'd forgotten they were there. "I don't feel pain like you do. Not anymore."

His eyes were somber as he said it, and her heart ached for whatever had made him resistant to pain.

"You won't have the seizures anymore, as long as you Change often enough to keep your bear happy. You should be good for another week now."

"You said you were going to help me, and you did." She nuzzled her face against his chest again and sighed. "You followed through on your promise. I thought I was lost. I thought my days were numbered and that I would only have a little time left here with you." It was scary to get her hopes up about the pain and sickness really being over. "Are you sure I won't have the seizures anymore?"

His heartbeat was solid and steady against her cheek. "I'm positive."

A flood of relief washed through her, and her knees buckled. Brighton held her tighter as she squeezed her eyes closed and relished in the revelation that she was going to live. That Connor hadn't killed her slowly like she'd thought. Brighton had been patient. He'd been tender when they'd made love and drawn her bear out of hiding. He'd made her animal feel safe enough to reveal herself.

"You said Connor claimed me and whoever did that decided the crew I'd belong to."

Brighton's heart rate bolted into a gallop against her cheek.

"Will I belong to the Ashe Crew now?"

"I suppose you can choose since your mate is dead."

"He was never my mate. Turning me didn't earn him that title. Maybe by your laws or traditions, or whatever, but not to me. And if the choice is mine, I want to be where you are. I choose the Ashe Crew."

She chose Brighton, though she still wasn't bold enough to tell him that out loud.

The soft hum sounded, just barely above her senses, and she snuggled closer. He did that when he was satisfied, and now, she adored that almost-tone. Before she could chicken out, she pushed her toes against the pebbly river bottom and pressed her lips against his.

Brighton's mouth softened against hers in an instant, his fingers entangling in her damp hair as he spun them slowly in the gentle current. He reached underwater and pulled the back of her knee until her leg wrapped around his hips, and before she could even plead with him, he slipped into her. She gasped at how good he felt, at how well they fit together, and angled her hips so that the next thrust of his thick shaft bumped against the sensitive spot he'd discovered earlier.

He cupped her ass, holding her as he pushed into her again and again. The water rippled with their movement, and her breasts mashed against his stony chest as he drew her firmly against him. Arms around his neck, she arched against him and met him stroke for stroke as pressure built inside of her, begging release. Soft, helpless moans escaped her lips, which only seemed to spur Brighton on faster. The muscles in his arms were flexed and hard, trembling as he tumbled toward orgasm with her. His breath came in pants as he kissed her shoulder, just above where Connor had bitten her back. Brighton's teeth grazed her skin, and a mixture of pleasure and fear of that pain again consumed her.

Brighton clamped down, his teeth pressing against her sensitive flesh, just shy of piercing her. She threw her head back and whispered his name over and over as release pounded through her. Brighton bit down harder as he came inside her, warmth filling her in pulsing streams. But just as she thought he'd sink his teeth into her neck muscle, he eased back and kissed her there instead.

Everly trembled from scalp to toes as her body was wracked with aftershocks. And when she found her legs too wobbly to hold her weight, Brighton scooped her up and carried her out of the water.

Water droplets clung to the ends of the dark hair that hung forward in his face. His eyes were the color of evergreens again, but they didn't land on her. Instead, he stared straight ahead, as if he was throwing all of his concentration to where he walked. Everly frowned and wrapped her arms around his neck.

"You wanted to bite me back there, didn't you?" she asked softly.

"No." The tone of the word sounded odd, even as a whisper. A muscle in his jaw twitched, and his shoulders relaxed as he carried her around an old mossy log in the middle of the path. "Yes. My bear wants to claim you."

"And I'm not really yours until you do what Connor did to me? Until you claim me?"

"I won't do that to you again. You've been through enough."

"Your bear wants me, but you don't?"

"Didn't say that, Ever," he rasped out. With a long, steady breath, he added, "I want you, too."

"Someday, if I asked you to claim me…would you?"

Trouble shadowed his eyes as he stared straight ahead. "It'll hurt, and you've been hurt by our kind enough. We're fine the way we are."

"Fine," she repeated.

But she wanted to be more than fine with him.

She wanted to nurture the love that was building between them. Brighton looked upset now, though, and whether it was from the thought of an uncomfortable conversation about a commitment that was more than he wanted, or at the idea of sinking his teeth into her and causing her that type of pain again, she couldn't tell.

All Everly knew was that, suddenly, *fine* didn't seem like enough.

# TEN

In the following days, Brighton's cabin became a sanctuary. It was an escape from the hard parts of real life. Everly could ignore the fact that she couldn't afford her rent or that a payment on her medical bills would be due soon. She could ignore the twenty missed calls from Momma and the texts that called her names and then begged forgiveness in a never-ending cycle that spoke volumes about whether she was drunk or sober at the time she sent them. Everly could ignore everything when she was tucked away, safe and sound, in Brighton's arms and home.

That was, until it became painfully apparent that

Brighton had bigger problems with his bear than he'd let on.

As time wore on, she began tracking his Changes. It wasn't because she wanted to pry into his private life, but because she was worried. The first night they'd spent together after her first Change, he'd left her bed in the middle of the night and returned an hour later. She was a light sleeper and was concerned, but he smiled grimly, kissed her on the forehead, tucked her against his chest and fell asleep, so she thought nothing was amiss. He'd said he had to Change more often, so this was something she would just have to get used to.

But the next night, he left her bed three times, and the next night, four. And during the day, when she wanted to spend that time getting to know everything about the man she was falling in love with, his eyes would churn silver, and he'd slip into the woods without a word of explanation.

It was apparent that quiet Brighton was battling demons she hadn't any guess at.

She offered to wash breakfast dishes, hoping that if he just relaxed while she worked, she would get a few extra minutes with him. Brighton plucked beautiful notes from an old guitar as he reclined in a dining chair. It was a song she recognized from the radio, so she hummed the tune along with the music as she threw a bowl of orange peels he'd used to squeeze fresh juice this morning into the wastebasket. She didn't have an amazing voice like his brother had when she'd heard them play at Sammy's Bar, but she could hold a tune. She used to sing lullabies to Momma when she was drunk as a skunk and begging for them. It struck her as backward, the child having to sing to the adult, but that was just how it had been growing up.

Everly frowned into the sink as she rinsed their plates off. She'd been weighed down with Momma's disappointment before she'd met Brighton, but she felt differently about that relationship now. She was more confident in herself and suspected Momma only said heinous things to make herself feel better. Brighton didn't like her, though he'd never met Momma. Everly could tell. His eyes would go dead every time she mentioned her, and yesterday he'd told her that Momma was wrong about her. That she wasn't a failure or a disappointment. She wasn't a whore. She was just someone who got the short end of the stick as far as parental units were concerned.

Everly had thought about it all day yesterday when she'd been waiting for Brighton to come home from a long Change. Perhaps he was right. The insults she'd absorbed from Momma for all these years had altered the way she saw herself. Everly had grown up feeling useless, but she wasn't. Brighton had showed her she was worthwhile. And his unending compliments rang much truer than Momma's veiled insults ever had. With her shifter instincts, she could tell the difference now.

Someday she was going to call Momma back, but when she did, that relationship would be different, or it wouldn't be anything at all. Brighton made her feel strong enough to lay down boundaries, and never again would she endure insults or let anyone step on her just to make their shitty day better. Nice people didn't act like that, and from here on, Everly was bound and determined that she would only allow nice people to play a part in her life. Her near death experience had taught her a lot, and one of those lessons was that life was too damned short to be a leaf in someone else's storm.

Happy with the revelation, she sang a few words

and soaped up a sponge, then scrubbed a bowl. When she looked up from the drying rack of dishes to ask Brighton if he wanted to go for a walk with her later, he had the most peculiar look in his eyes. He sat frozen except for his fingers, which moved gracefully across the frets of his guitar. His head canted and a curious smile ghosted his lips.

*You have a beautiful voice*, he mouthed. His voice had gone after a long conversation over breakfast.

She beamed as heat flooded her cheeks. Dropping her gaze, she wrung the sponge out into the sink, rinsed the suds from her hands, then leaned her back against the counter. "Flatterer."

*Would you sing that song if Denison and I played it at Sammy's Bar one night?*

"Me? Oh, no. I can sing in front of you, but in front of a crowd is...well...I can't imagine myself doing that."

*Even if I was right there with you?*

Everly shrugged, flattered that he thought she was good enough. Just the idea of performing in front of people made her veins run cold. It sure was nice that he'd asked, but it wouldn't ever be something that would come to fruition.

Brighton jerked his chin, beckoning her, and settled the guitar against the wall beside him. He held out his hands, and she sank into his lap.

*Do you know how special your bear is?*

She shook her head. "She's albino. I've never seen pictures of an albino bear. I've seen blond ones, but not pure white, like me. Makes me weird, huh?"

Brighton pulled over the scribbled up notepad that sat waiting on the table, then wrote, *Not weird, no. But you're special in other ways. You're submissive. That shyness you feel around other people? That personality trait manifested in your animal as well. I think that, coupled with the trauma of how you were Turned, is what made your bear afraid to come out. All of her ideal conditions had to be met, and she had to feel safe before she revealed herself.*

"Submissive?" That didn't sound good. She wanted to be strong—a strong partner for Brighton, who deserved nothing less.

His smile deepened, and he brushed a strand of her hair from her face. He swallowed hard, then forced a whisper. "Submissive isn't a bad thing. You'll be the only one in the Ashe Crew. Tagan will shit himself, he'll be so happy. He's got his hands full of a crew full of dominant bears. You'll bring balance to us."

"What does submissive mean? Weak?"

"Never weak." He shook his head and leveled her a serious look. "Never. You just won't want to fight like the rest of us do. You'll keep your head during skirmishes. Your bear is a peacemaker." His voice lowered to nothing. *I knew the first time I smelled you that you would be a balm. My bear settles around you, and he's a monster.*

"Not a monster," she murmured, brushing her thumb down the short, dark stubble on his face and along the scar on his throat. "He's perfect for me."

Brighton dropped his gaze, but not before she saw the shame in his eyes. Carefully, he pulled the palm of her hand to his lips and kissed it for a long time. When he looked up again, his eyes roiled with liquid silver, and she knew she was losing him to the woods again.

Pursing her lips, she hugged him tight, resting her chin against his shoulder and wishing for a few more minutes. "You hold too much inside, and for what? Whatever you're going through will only make me respect you more. You are full of poison because you don't talk about what makes your bear like this. I can see you getting worse. I can see your pain, but you refuse to share it with me." Her eyes rimmed with tears as she eased back and cupped her hands around his neck.

Brighton wouldn't look at her anymore, and his mouth had settled into the same grim line he'd worn the first day she'd talked to him at that diner.

Her heart was breaking into pieces, just like it did every time he was forced to Change because of the ghosts he was fighting.

"I'm here, Brighton. I love you, and I'll always be here."

He shook his head slowly back and forth, in denial of the relief she offered. If he'd only tell her what was wrong, and how she could help him, she'd gladly take on any burden he would allow her to. He gripped her wrists and pulled her grasp from his neck, then stood and left the kitchen. The front door slammed closed a moment later, and she strode for the window to watch him leave like she always did. Pushing back the curtains with her fingertips, she followed his escape with her eyes as tears spilled from them and streaked down her cheeks. He removed his shirt, putting his scars on display. His muscles worked and flexed under his skin as he moved, too graceful to be human. At the edge of the tree line, he paused and turned back. His chin was lowered and his gaze steady, as if he could see her through the kitchen window, all the way from across the clearing. Heartbreak swam in his eyes, and he gritted his teeth. In the final moment before he turned back for the woods, he looked sick about leaving her like this.

She couldn't force him to open up, though.

All Everly could do was hope that someday he would trust her enough to share his burdens.

****

It slayed her that Brighton had to spend so much time alone in the woods just for a few hours in his human skin. She'd begun to form an idea over the time she'd been here, and this morning, she'd had enough. Everly followed the scent trail Brighton had left. She couldn't just sit in the cabin waiting for him when she knew he was hurting. Not anymore. She was in this too deep, cared about him too much not to take desperate measures.

This was the second attempt of the day to

Change. This morning, she'd been terrified and stank of fear as she'd followed him into the woods, then attempted to Change when he was in sight. Brighton as a bear had been worried, pacing frantically as she forced herself through the pain of an unnecessary transformation. It had taken a long time, and she was only able to remain a bear for half an hour at most, but she'd done it. And dammit, she was going to continue doing it so he wouldn't be alone with whatever he was carrying anymore.

Brighton stood beside a young spruce tree, shaking his head as if he'd just Turned and was trying to rid himself of the last tingles. Tugging at her shirt, she pulled it over her head and folded it neatly. Her jeans and panties followed, each folded into the pile that sat on a flat boulder. Hopefully, the bugs wouldn't find them, but just in case, she'd try to remember to shake them out when she Turned back and redressed.

Brighton's eyes landed on her, still silver from Turning and not yet settled into the almond color he donned when in his furry form for a while. He approached slowly, shaking his head like one of those caged bears at a zoo.

She wouldn't be warned off, though. Closing her eyes, she imagined her bear, called to her, opened her mind and her middle to allow a metamorphosis she was only beginning to understand. Her bear, not yet ready after this morning, fought the transition, and the pain was excruciating. Sweat beaded her forehead, and she gritted her teeth and grunted at the invisible blows she received. Her insides were on fire, but she fell to her knees and arched her neck back, hands out and palms to the sky as her bones began to break.

She lay crumpled on the forest floor, prickly pine needles poking her muzzle when it was done. She'd slept well last night, but now she felt as if she were exhausted. Weakly, she pushed herself up onto all fours and stumbled toward Brighton.

He was frozen, and a look of utter confusion had morphed his features. He blasted steam from his mouth in the cool air. When at last she reached him, he bowed his head and rubbed his body down her ribs, and then around to the other side. A silent question that asked, *why would she bother for me?*

Everly bumped his shoulder and tried to put on a brave face, but her body was revolting, and there was no masking the scent of her pain. Brighton circled her tightly, but there was no danger to protect her from. He scanned the woods around them, eyes intense as if he was preparing himself to defend her. And within moments, her Change began again. The birds in the canopy above flocked into the air at her roar of agony. And when the tingling in her nerve endings dulled, she redressed gingerly and followed Brighton numbly through the woods until he turned back into the man she loved and carried her back home.

He didn't say anything. Hadn't all day, but when he settled her onto the porch, he whispered, "I'm no good for you, Ever. I never will be."

"That's horseshit, Brighton. You're mine, and I'm not giving up on you. You can't live your life like this alone. So until your bear gives you relief, I'll follow you, and I'll Change with you until I can't anymore."

His chest rose as he inhaled deeply and searched her face. "I need time alone."

His need to escape ripped hurt through her middle. Those were the worst words she'd ever heard strung together. She knew what it meant. His first step in letting her go. Maybe she was pushing too hard, too fast. Or perhaps he didn't feel the devotion that she did. He'd saved her, after all, and she owed him everything. She, on the other hand, hadn't done anything for him.

He squeezed her hand, then kissed her forehead and sauntered off toward the barn without looking back.

She swallowed the urge to follow him—to hug him and tell him how much she'd fallen in love with him over the last week and beg him not to push her away. But if he didn't care for her in that way, what was the point? She'd only be more hurt in the end.

A sob clogged her throat, and she gulped it down. She crossed her arms over her chest to ward off the cold that was seeping into her and traced the wood grain of the log walls of the cabin with her eyes.

This place was only a paradise if Brighton was happy, too.

And clearly, her being here wasn't bringing him joy like it was for her. Maybe it was time to get back to the real world and give Brighton the space he seemed to need. She'd read in a library book once, if something truly belonged to a person, they had to set it free and allow it a chance to come back.

Maybe that's what she'd been doing wrong with

Brighton. Forcing him. Forcing this.

Inside, she cried as she packed her duffle bag. On the bed they shared, she stacked the clothes he'd so thoughtfully packed for her that first day when he didn't know her.

So much had changed since then.

She'd discovered what she was, but more than that, she'd discovered she could be strong. She would go back to the real world a different person. One who could hold her head up a little higher. Maybe she wouldn't be so shy around new people, and maybe someday she'd get the courage to sing karaoke at a bar in town, just to prove to herself that she was as brave as Brighton thought she was. She could walk down the street not staring at the cracks in the concrete and look up at the world instead—look ahead to what life was going to bring her.

Brighton had given her life back. Perhaps not the life she'd left behind, but one where she could be okay eventually. One where the animal inside of her could bring her confidence, not kill her slowly.

God, she would miss him. Just thinking about going back to Saratoga without him gutted her. She dashed the back of her hands across her lashes until they were dry, shoved the final bag of toiletries into the side zipper of her bag, then fastened it up and pulled it across her shoulder.

She looked back at the house, memorizing every detail. The warped floorboards that had been worn smooth and shining. The vase of late-season wildflowers she'd arranged on the dining table. The small kitchen where she and Brighton had spent hours cooking together, laughing and flirting, touching…kissing. She'd already memorized his lips and the way they felt against her skin. As long as she lived, she would never forget that. She committed to memory the rustic furniture and a dark, ethereal painting of logging machinery that hung from the biggest wall in the living room. The signature in the bottom read *Brooke* in a looping, barely legible scrawl.

This place was where she'd found herself in so many ways.

The hollow sound of the closing door behind her made her feel empty inside. It had to be the loneliest sound in the whole world. She hefted her bag to the old tire swing that clung to the branches of a giant tree out front.

The rope swing creaked out an easy rhythm as Everly pressed the heels of her boots into the dirt and swung in the breeze as she waited for Brighton to decide he'd had enough time away from her. She didn't want to rush him for a ride back into town, so she waited patiently outside and hoped he would come back in time to take her back to her apartment before dark.

Brighton came out of the barn, and his attention settled immediately on the bag beside her. His expression turned grim in an instant. When he dragged his gaze back to hers, his eyes were clear and green instead of the silver she'd grown to expect.

She slowed the swing as he approached. His strong hand gripped her neck, massaged it with a gentle touch, then disappeared. He pushed her lower back, and she lifted her legs to allow the old tire to carry her through the air.

"You can't be Changing with me like that anymore," he whispered.

"I know. It's not what you want."

"No, I just can't stand to watch you hurt like that. You have to stop."

She didn't answer. Instead, she nodded and

watched a flock of birds fly across the sky. She was leaving anyway, so what did it matter?

"I was sixteen."

Confused, she twisted in the oversize tire and dragged her feet against the dirt to stop her trajectory. "What?"

"Don't look at me while I'm telling you, or I won't be able to do this."

Her eyes went wide, and she turned back around. From here, she could hear his heartbeat, and it was pounding like the fast-rhythm base in some techno song. She wanted to hold him while he spilled his secrets, but it wasn't his way.

He swallowed audibly and continued, "My twin brother, Denison, and I were home alone for the first time, and people...humans...came and took us. We fought, but they injected us with something that suppressed our animals. I woke up in this sterile room to this awful sound in my ears. That sound, I came to realize, was my own screams as they cut into me without anesthesia. That was the first time of many. Denison's bear was more manageable and took less injections to control him, while I took twice the dosage. My bear had always been angrier, stronger, and I wanted to fight what was happening to me. They said Denison would be their breeder. They planned on kidnapping a she-bear and studying their reproductive habits, as well as our genetics. They tested on my brother, but it was all internal, and they gave him something that repressed his memories."

Brighton's whisper sounded tortured as he pushed her again, and Everly could hear the scratch of him rubbing the scruff on his face with his free hand.

"I was called the Tissue Sample. That's what they referred to me as. No name, just, 'take the Tissue Sample into the operating room. He's healed enough to go again.' You've probably noticed how fast we heal. So, they would bring me to the brink of death, give me a few hours, and I'd be ready for their scalpels again."

"Oh, Brighton," Everly whispered as agony washed over her.

"I remember everything. Every cut. Every strip of flesh they took from me because they kept me awake. The same IV that kept my bear inside of me, shredding me from the inside out but never able to protect me, held medicines that kept me still but awake for the operations. Some bullshit about pain tolerance testing." His whisper cracked and he walked around the tire and fell to his knees in front of her. "I don't want you to leave, but I understand if you have to. This is what I am. This is what you're getting yourself into. I'll always be broken." His fingers clutched her jeans and his forehead rested against her knees.

"Finish it, Brighton. Tell it to me, every bit of it, and be done with carrying this alone."

Slowly, he rubbed his face against her pants, and tiny dark splotches spotted them where his eyes had touched. "I saw Denison sometimes. I'd call out to him if I was able, but it was like he didn't see me. He didn't see anything, he was so drugged up. The nurses and doctors would move him to a different testing area or back to his cell, and he'd follow them easily, while I fought everything. I stopped healing as quickly by the second day. They'd carved on me all night, and they seemed satisfied from the strips they'd taken from my torso and leg. A man named Reynolds headed all the operations and seemed to be in charge, and I remember when he told me they were going to start carving out my insides, I got sick in my cell. He watched me retching, and then thanked me for my sacrifice in the name of science, and I was terrified. I was just a fucking kid, worried about what was happening to my brother, and if I'd ever see my parents and sister again. The next surgery, Reynolds took my voice. He removed something from my neck and said they wanted to study how I was able to talk and growl at the same time. And I wanted to die. I prayed for it. At first I prayed to pass out from the pain at each operation, but then, on the last day, I just wanted the pain to end."

He lifted his silver gaze to Everly's. She'd never seen this kind of heartbreak in a man's eyes, and it killed her to hear what he'd gone through. But she had to be brave now because he was finally letting her in. She stroked his dark locks until he found his whispered voice again.

"I was being sliced when I saw Denison that last day. He had that vacant look in his eyes that said he'd been drugged heavily, and I expected him to just walk on past the room I was in without seeing me like he always did. I watched him because I was scared it would be the last time I'd ever see him, and it was the only way I could say goodbye to my brother. But he looked up. It was the first life I'd seen in him, and his eyes landed right one me." Brighton cast his attention toward the woods. "He Changed. I don't know how he bypassed the drugs, but he killed the doctors who were escorting him down the hall, and he shredded the doctors who were working on me while he was at it. Reynolds ran, the fucking coward, and Denison let me out of my straps. He ripped the IV out of my arm, and alarms were going off so loud, I thought my eardrums would burst. Red lights flashing and panic as the doctors tried to flee, and we killed them. Men and women, it didn't matter to us. We killed the entire team that had worked on us, one by one. Denison made a bad kill. A slow one on a woman I'd seen with him the most. Later he told me he didn't' know why he'd let her bleed out like that, but I'd watched him as she died. He looked at her with such hatred. She'd done something awful to him. He just couldn't remember what had his bear despising her so much. Denison passed out before we made it out of the building, and I was in bad shape. Still bleeding. The pain had stopped at some point like I'd gotten used to it, but I had no idea where we were. It took me a full day to get us back home. Denison came back with little memory of the experience we'd been through, and I came back completely broken. I came home to nightmares and a bear that revolted after being suppressed and tortured. I do my best to hide what those doctors did to me, and when I can't stop the Changes, I come here and hide away from the Ashe Crew so they won't see how fucked up I really am."

Everly slid through the tire swing and fell to her knees in front of him, then hugged him to her, clenching her hands against his back. He'd found jeans in the barn, but his torso was bare, exposing all of those horrifying marks. She knew how fast she healed, and to make thick, red scars like that, those doctors had to have taken huge strips of flesh from him. She couldn't imagine the pain from one that stretched halfway around his body, much less the fifteen that went from under his arm to his thigh like zebra stripes.

"Is that why you don't like to whisper?"

"It reminds me of what was done. I haven't used it much since it happened. It's painful, but it sometimes sets my bear off, too. The whisper didn't really feel worth it. Not until you."

"What happened to Reynolds?"

"He came after me and Denison and the rest of our crew a few months ago. We got out with the help of the Gray Backs and Boarlanders, but just barely. Denison dragged Reynolds into the woods after the fight and pinned him against a tree, and I...I killed him. It should've given me closure, right? To kill the last man left alive who'd tortured me. But instead, it dredged up all the things I'd gone through in that lab. And now, my bear is out of control, just from seeing the man again." His voice rasped to nothing and he winced.

Gently, she lifted his chin and cupped his face in her palms. Searching his eyes, she murmured, "I'm not going anywhere. If you thought this was going to scare me off, you're wrong. It has only made me love you more."

His eyes went round with disbelief and his breath caught. His face crumpled with emotion, and he pressed his forehead against her chest, hiding his face from her. "Say it again," he rasped out in a barely audible whisper.

"I love you, Brighton Beck. You are the strongest, sweetest, most amazing man I've ever met, and you're all mine. My mate, my man. You've only tethered me to you more by letting me in. I love you. I *love* you." Her voice cracked as she repeated it once more and nuzzled the top of his head as she rocked him gently.

Brighton's shoulders sagged as if a hundred pounds of weight had been lifted from him. Maybe it had been.

She didn't know how to fix him, but she knew she wouldn't stop trying to help until she drew her last breath.

Brighton had survived something horrific and had still taken time out of his life to save her, even as he was struggling with his own gritty experiences. It took a great and selfless man to do something like that. She was going to show him just how coveted he was, just how worth it he was.

And as she rocked him in the dirt beneath the old tire swing on that cool September morning, she realized that she'd never felt this way about anyone. Hadn't known this type of love existed.

Because he'd been brave enough to allow her in, her heart would belong to him for always.

# ELEVEN

Everly fidgeted with the corner of the dishcloth in her hands and checked the window to the front yard for the hundredth time. Brighton had said he had errands to run in town, but that had been hours ago, and if her calculations were correct, it was past time for him to Change.

Her imagination had run away with her as it concocted stories of him turning into a grizzly on Bridge Avenue in front of everyone.

Brighton usually did dishes. He seemed to prefer the routine of them, but she was so nervous she'd already tidied his cabin from top to bottom and made an entire vat of homemade chicken noodle soup. For something to preoccupy her mind, the clean dishes that decorated the drying rack were getting a twice over.

The soft rumble of Brighton's truck sounded from far away, pricking her ears. "Thank God." She rinsed the last plate and yanked the dishtowel from her shoulder, then bolted for the front porch. Pacing, she wrung her hands, her eyes never leaving the gravel drive that wound through the trees beyond the clearing of the front yard.

Her shoulders relaxed the moment she saw Brighton behind the wheel. From here, she could tell his eyes weren't even silver. Perhaps he'd Changed on the way in then. She jogged out to meet him as he parked in the front meadow. His smile was contagious as he opened the door and caught her hug. Lifting her off her feet, he spun her slowly as she planted kisses all over his face.

"I missed you, silly bear. I was worried something had happened."

"I got you something," he rasped out, then reached for the bench seat of his truck and pulled out a bag from a clothing boutique she recognized from

Saratoga.

Her face went slack with shock as he settled her on her feet. "You bought me this?"

*Open it*, he mouthed.

She tore out the tissue paper and pulled out a pink and white floral dress with a matching cardigan. A pair of beige flats were in the bottom of the bag.

*I checked the sizes of your clothes and shoes before I went into town this morning.* Brighton's emerald-colored eyes were so open and hopeful looking that she nestled against his chest and hugged him tight.

"No one has ever bought me anything like this." She fingered the soft cotton fabric and smiled up at him. "It's beautiful."

*You like it?*

"I love it. You want me to try it on?"

A soft smile graced his lips, then faded as he nodded his head seriously.

"Okay, give me a minute."

In the bedroom, the mirror must've been feeling extra generous. Her dark under-eye circles had all but disappeared, and already she didn't look as emaciated. Partially thanks to Brighton being a wonderful cook and feeding her like clockwork, but also because she had a healthy balance between her human side and her animal side now. She hadn't had a single seizure since the first time she'd Changed. Even her hair looked shinier, and her lips looked pinker. Her cheeks had color to them, and her eyes were a clear and happy blue. Emotion choked her up, and she looked away before the waterworks started. Brighton had done this for her.

She dressed slowly, then smoothed the wrinkles from the full knee-length skirt. The top was fitted with delicate straps that made her collar bones look quite lovely. The cream-colored cardigan matched the flats she slipped onto her feet, and when she looked in the mirror again, she felt like a princess. He'd imagined her in this dress and had picked out exactly the dress she would have adored on a manikin while window shopping.

"You look beautiful," Brighton whispered from the open doorway. He leaned on the frame, arms crossed over his chest, shoulders relaxed as he raked his approving gaze down her figure.

"I feel beautiful." She stepped lightly to him and held his hands in her own. "You make me feel good about myself."

He lifted his chin, pride evident in his face as he nodded. "I bought you the dress for a reason."

"What reason?"

"My brother is marrying his mate tonight. I want to take you."

She canted her head and smiled shyly. "Like a date?"

"Always my date," he said without hesitation. "You're my mate, Everly Moore. I've been waiting to show you off to my crew, and now, I think you're ready."

Her first reaction was happiness, but as concern over his bear invaded her excited thoughts, she began to fret. He'd told her all about the Ashe Crew, and late last night, in the bed they shared together, he'd admitted that he was in hiding because of his troublesome inner animal. He hadn't wanted his crew to worry.

"What about your Changes? Will you be able to control them while we're there?"

A slow smile split his face until his straight, white teeth stood out against his designer facial scruff. "You want to hear a secret?" he asked, ducking around her, then sitting on the edge of the bed.

"I always want to hear your secrets," she answered honestly.

"I haven't Changed since I told you about my past."

"But Brighton, that was more than a day ago." Hope bloomed in her chest, warming her from the inside out until her skin tingled.

"Telling you all of that helped. I didn't have to leave you at all last night, and this morning, I just felt different. There's less fire inside of me. My bear feels…settled around you."

She clenched her teeth against the urge to cry and tackled him onto the bed. "Did I save you back?" she asked on a breath. Straddling him, she rested the palms of her hands on his chest.

The corner of his lips lifted as he ran his hands down her arms and circled his fingers around her wrists, as if he wanted to keep her touch right where it was against his thrumming heartbeat.

"Yeah, Ever. You saved me back."

****

Nerves fluttered around inside of Everly, causing tiny earthquakes in her stomach. Tonight she would meet the Ashe Crew. Brighton had told her so much about each one of them, she felt like she already knew them, but they didn't know her. She wanted them to like her for Brighton's sake. He would move back to his trailer in the Asheland Mobile Park soon, and the people here were like his extended family. Tagan, the alpha, his pregnant mate, Brooke. Kellen, the crew's second, and his falcon shifter mate, Skyler. Denison and Danielle. Haydan, Bruiser, and Drew, the bachelors of a crew who lived here and worked as lumberjacks on a jobsite in the mountains near the community.

Everly wanted to fit in with them so badly her hands shook and her palms were sweaty. She'd never been good at first impressions. Her shy awkwardness always sucked the fun out of meeting new people and filled her with anxiety. It didn't help either that the submissive bear in her middle was telling her to flee the dominant, apex predator shifters who stood at the end of the dirt road that led through the trailer park.

Brighton squeezed her hand from their place hidden in the night shadows of the woods that lined the trailer park. He shifted his weight as if he was nervous about seeing his friends again. She straightened the collar of his button down shirt and patted her palms lightly against his chest. "Perfect," she whispered.

He kissed her forehead, then rested his cheek against her hair as they watched Denison strut down the road with his bride-to-be thrown over his shoulder. Their aisle was a dusty gravel street that bisected two rows of trailers. Strands of lights had been strung up everywhere. Along the paths and cracked sidewalks, on porches and opened truck beds were candles flickering inside of glass jelly jars. It was stunning and so much more than she'd imagined when Brighton had described his home.

By Brighton's descriptions, Everly recognized the group of friends who were gathered near a bonfire. Brooke with her flowing blond hair and belly swollen with child, Skyler with her dark hair and striking green eyes. Tagan, who stood stoically with a proud smile on his face. Kellen with his scarred face and dark eyes that stayed on his mate, Skyler. Denison, who looked just like Brighton, only with lighter hair and gray eyes. Drew with his shoulder-length blond hair, who looked like some rugged

Viking from ancient times. Haydan with his tattoos and shaved head, and Bruiser with his laughing, almond-colored eyes and shoulders the width of a doublewide. This group of friends already felt so familiar, but...

Brighton pulled her hand and mouthed, *You ready?*

Panic flared in her chest, freezing her breath. There was so much pressure. This would be her Crew now, and if they didn't like her, she was shit out of luck. Everly shook her head. "I can't do this."

*You can. They will love you.*

"Brighton, I can't go in there, right in the middle of a surprise wedding, and take attention away from the bride like that. This is Danielle's moment. It doesn't feel right. I don't want that to be the first memory I make with the Ashe Crew.

His frown lifted, and his expression relaxed. His words were soft as the breeze here in the dark. "Wait here then if it'll make this easier for you. Come out when you are ready, and I'll make the proper introductions. Don't be nervous, Ever. You have me with you. Always."

She heaved a sigh of relief and nodded.

Brighton kissed her knuckles with a sexy, crooked smile, then turned and strode for his friends. She watched in awe as he endured slaps on the back and rough hugs, and all the while, his eyes stayed green and his bear hidden. She was so damned proud of him. He'd carried a heavy burden for so long, and then been brave enough to share himself with her. This had been his reward—normalcy. Brighton pressed his forehead against Danielle's, and the woman smiled through glistening tears that spilled over. Then he did the same to his brother.

The ceremony was short and sweet as honey. The bride was glowing, and Denison looked like he couldn't be happier, positioned in front of his alpha, and flanked by his mate and his brother.

After it was finished and the bride was kissed, when the hugs and congratulations were through and the crew had settled around the bonfire, Everly found her bravery. She smoothed the wrinkles from her dress, then stepped from the shadows.

Brighton's eyes landed on her, and a slow smile took his face as he twitched his head for her to come closer. He met her halfway, intertwined his fingers in hers, and pulled her to the edge of the bonfire light where the Ashe Crew had gone quiet and still.

She cleared her throat and searched their faces, the people she would be bound to if they accepted her. "Hello." Her voice came out weak, and heat flooded her cheeks.

"Holy shit," Bruiser muttered. His nostrils flared, and he took a step toward her. "Are you a submissive grizzly?"

"Yes," she squeaked out.

Brighton rubbed her back, and she dropped her gaze to the ground, unable to hold eye contact with the shifters who were filling the air between them with something weighty and just above her senses. "I'm Everly."

Strong arms went around her and lifted her from the ground until her back cracked. Denison was giving her a literal interpretation of a bear hug. "Damn, girl. We thought you were gonna die. It's good to see you in the land of the living."

"What?" she asked as he set her down. She wobbled, but caught her balance just as Tagan hugged her shoulders.

"Brighton asked us to come over to see if I could do anything to help you. I take it you've Changed now? You look much better than the last time we saw you. We...well, we feared the worst for you." Denison twitched his head toward his brother. "And for Brighton."

The Ashe Crew passed her around, shaking her hand, patting her back, squeezing her arm, and gently hugging her, all the while each of the shifters inhaled her scent unabashedly. She didn't understand. This was supposed to be harder.

When she'd been thoroughly embraced, she settled her shoulder blades against Brighton's chest and stared questioningly at the band of friends. "I thought I would have to pass some werebear tests to be accepted."

Brooke's smile was so genuinely happy, Everly instantly liked her. "No tests from us. If Brighton picked you, you must be special."

"Does everyone know who I am?" Everly asked. She couldn't lift her gaze to their eyes no matter how hard she tried.

"Tagan told us," Skyler explained. "You're Connor's claim."

Those three words drew the hair up on the back of her neck. Everly shook her head as Brighton tightened his grip on her upper arms. "I never belonged to Connor." She dragged her eyes up to Tagan and clenched her hands. "I'm Brighton's mate."

"Good," Tagan said, lifting his chin in approval. "It seems we have a lot to celebrate tonight then. We'll do your initiation in the morning. Drew, break out that booze, man. Brighton and Haydan, this shindig needs food." He jerked a thumb toward a grill to the side of the fire. Behind that was an unstained, rough wooden table with piles of groceries stacked on it.

"I can help," she whispered to Brighton.

He nodded, then bent down and kissed her lips. He took soft, small sips, then eased back and mouthed, *I told you they'd like you.*

A grin cracked open her face, and her cheeks burned with shyness. She'd never kissed a man in front of an audience before, but when she turned, no one seemed to notice but Brooke, who was watching them with a soft look on her face.

Skyler had settled into Kellen's lap and was nuzzling his cheek, and Denison and Danielle were standing to the side, talking quietly between kisses. The other boys were apparently having an asparagus eating competition, and she laughed at their trash talk. The smelliest piss-off at the end of the night would determine the winner.

Drew handed her a Dixie cup of what looked like red wine, and she thanked him, then slurped it down like a shot in hopes of ridding herself of the nervous flutters that had her hands shaking and her stomach quivering. Drew plucked the empty from her hand and refilled it from a box with a spigot at the bottom. She giggled as he handed the cup back to her, overflowing and splashing dark drops into the dirt near her feet.

Denison pulled a trio of beers from an old cooler by the table, handed one to Danielle and another to Brighton. The brothers popped the tops and tinked the bottles together.

"It's good to have you back, brother," Denison said.

Brighton nodded and took a long swig before draping an arm over Everly's shoulders and pulling her against his side. *It's good to be back.*

Denison gripped the back of his head and shook him a few times, then shoved him and rejoined his new wife by the fire. Everly made her way to the table and took up food prep with Haydan as Brighton prepared the grill. She wasn't comfortable joining in conversation quite yet, but as time ticked by, she settled into the easy connection between the people here. Laughter was constant, ribbing and light-hearted insults were tossed here and there, and the conversation flowed from one topic to the next with the ease of a crew that was happy with the family they'd built. A constant smile stayed on Everly's lips as she cut zucchinis, squash, onions, tomatoes, and mushrooms, then speared them with metal skewers.

Brighton came up behind her and nipped her earlobe before he took the plate of prepared food from in front of her and lined up the lanced vegetables on the grill. And when she glanced over at him, he was smiling in that absent way that likely matched her own happy expression.

Haydan talked constantly about how when season came again, they'd be up logging in the mountains above them, hitting numbers that a man named Damon Daye had hired them to do. Right now, he was listing all of the questionable decisions he and the other boys had made in the last week out of sheer boredom waiting for the season to start up next month. Mud wrestling, drinking contests, and someone had welded giant horseshoes they had to chuck at a log in the ground. Drew had rebuilt a skate ramp they'd destroyed a while back, and Bruiser broke his arm falling off. Though now, it was already healed again, and from the way he was snickering at Haydan's telling of it, Bruiser didn't regret the memory. They'd put an enormous tarp down a hill and sprayed it down with soap suds and water, and at the end, everyone went flying into the water of some nearby pond. That game had lasted a few straight days until Tagan almost got bit by a water moccasin.

Everly cleaned her hands on a paper towel and looked around at the animated faces, talking easily and laughing at something Denison had said.

One thing was for sure and for certain, there was never going to be a dull moment in this crew.

# TWELVE

Brighton opened the door to his trailer. He hadn't been here since the day he'd killed Reynolds, and even then, it was just for a few moments to pack necessities into a backpack before he blasted out of here and sought the safety of the cabin.

He'd expected it to smell rough, but when he opened up the fridge, he huffed air from his cheeks and leaned on the door. Cool, clean air hit his face. Nothing was inside, save condiments with long expiration dates. Denison must've come in here and cleaned out the place. His brother was solid like that, always dependable, always giving him what he needed before he knew he needed it.

A flash of Denison slamming Reynolds against the tree and tossing Brighton the ax to end his life flickered across his mind. His brother had been tortured at the hand of that monster too, and he could've taken revenge for himself, but he'd known, in that uncanny way of his, that Reynolds needed to die by Brighton's hand.

Damn, he was so glad Denison had found his mate in Danielle. He'd always liked her, always thought she'd been a steadying force for his brother. Tonight had been big. Tonight, Brighton had gained another sister.

He let the door to the fridge close and looked around at the tidy trailer. He ran his finger across the two-chair kitchen table and inspected it for dirt. Denison, that clean freak, had even dusted. Mom had instilled tidiness in them since they were cubs, but for whatever reason, Denison's bear required a clean den and a steady schedule, unlike Brighton's inner grizzly who thrived on chaos. He couldn't remember much about his life or who he'd been before he was tortured, but Brighton thought maybe his animal had always been a little wild. The cutting had just made him insane as well as feral.

He closed his eyes and searched inward. Oh, his bear was still there, like a hibernating giant waiting for something to wake him and release the titan, but it wasn't like before. Now, his animal side felt manageable. Everly had done that for him.

A soft knock sounded at the door, and he turned. His mate hesitated in the doorframe, shifting her weight as if she didn't know her place here. Brighton held out his hands in silent question. *What do you think?*

Two tentative steps, and she was inside his den. The real place his heart lived. The cabin was a good place to run to, but this old trailer was home.

"I grew up in a trailer park," she murmured softly, as if she didn't want to break the spell of this place.

*Yeah?*

She nodded and pulled a pink beach towel more tightly around her middle. The boys had nixed a hillbilly hot tub to celebrate Denison's nuptials on account of it taking too long to heat the water, and the boys were too drunk to be safe about it anyhow. Then Bruiser, jacked up on asparagus and boxed wine, got the idea they should all go skinny-dipping in the creek by moonlight. Most of them had been down to party, but Brooke, God bless that woman, had taken one look at Everly's terrified face and offered her a bathing suit. His alpha's mate even went a step further and told Everly she was going to wear a bathing suit, too.

Now, everyone had seen everyone in the nude here. Even utterly human Danielle had joined in on the occasional midnight skinny-dipping party. But Everly was different. She was new to this life and unsure of her place in the Ashe Crew. And if he was honest, her shyness and modesty only made him adore her more.

"This trailer park is way nicer than the one I lived in. Neighbors are pretty cool, too," she said with a self-conscious little shrug.

She was so fuckin' cute, it wasn't even fair. If she even knew how much she melted him, how much she locked his damned knees when she was around, she'd think he was a hopeless sap.

Her gorgeous eyes widened as she asked, "Can I look around?"

Oh. Right. Grand tour, and here he was just

staring at her like a weirdo. He showed her around. It wasn't much. Two bedrooms, two baths, only one of which actually worked because of the rampant plumbing problems up here. He was going to dig up the crushed pipes and replace them next week to keep the snakes out of the toilet bowl. Everly deserved a safe place after all she'd been through.

He couldn't stop watching her. Everly's nostrils flared, as if she was committing this place to memory. Or perhaps she smelled him all over his den. The absent smile on her lips was so damned sexy he couldn't keep from kissing her every time she got close enough.

"The girls have all spent time living in trailer ten-ten across the street," he whispered as he settled his shoulder blades across the doorframe to his bedroom. "Tagan said it's yours if you want it."

Everly dropped her gaze to the toe of his boot, and her shoulders slumped. "That's very kind."

"Or," he said, hooking a finger under her chin and lifting her gaze back to his. "You can stay here with me and make this place your home."

A hopeful smile brushed her lips. Her pert little nose scrunched up as her grin deepened. "You mean it?"

"Woman, I can't even stand the thought of you living across the street. That's how pathetically deep I am in this. I just wanted to give you space if you needed it. Some of the other women in our crew have had a hard time adjusting to this life. I don't want that for you. I want you to be happy." Brighton's voice caught at the pain of whispering. "I want to make you happy."

"You make me the happiest, silly bear." She pushed against his chest flirtatiously and leaned against the other side of the doorframe. "You want to see the swimsuit Brooke let me borrow?"

*Hell. Yes.*

Her lips lifted in a wicked smile as she pulled the towel away from her skin. A crimson red two-piece with tiny black polka-dots, and his dick instantly thumped against the seam of his jeans. Damn, she was beautiful, and the last week had been good to her. She had weight to gain yet, but the sickly thinness was nothing but a dim memory. She didn't look fragile anymore. Instead, she looked strong. And there was nothing on this earth sexier than a strong woman.

Just as he reached for her, a tremendous banging echoed down the side of the trailer. Bruiser, that twit, needed to learn to knock on a door.

"We're leaving!" Bruiser called out through the thin walls. "Quit fuckin' around in there and let's go." His voice went muffled. "Get it? Fuckin' around?"

"Shut up, man," Drew murmured from farther away, and Everly snickered and shook her head.

At least she found amusement in their antics. That would get her far here.

Brighton leaned forward and kissed her hard, then bit her lip just enough that she moaned. He slipped his hand down the front of her bathing suit bottoms and ran his finger through the slickness of her sex. She was always ready for him, always wet when they flirted, and he couldn't get over how lucky he'd gotten, falling for a woman like Everly. His brave little mate who wanted intimacy with him despite what Connor had done to her.

"Please," she begged on a breath.

"You wanna come on my hand?" he whispered against her ear.

A nod, and he checked the front door. Bruiser would probably barge in if he didn't finish her in about a minute, so he pulled Everly inside his bedroom and pressed her against the wall. He slid his finger into her, then a second on the next stroke, careful to touch her clit. Damn, she was so sensitive there he had to be careful or he'd hurt her if he lost his head and got too rough. When he cupped her on the next stroke, she tossed her head against the wall and moaned. He swallowed the sound of her pleasure so they wouldn't attract the wrath of the crew. He pushed his tongue past her lips and tasted her. Three more strokes, and she pulsed around his fingers and clutched onto his back, nails curved like talons against him, and sexy, helpless little noises in her throat. He'd never get tired of her response to his touch. Not ever.

God, he was so turned on, he could probably blow his load just rubbing up against her right now.

"Brighton, Everly!" Bruiser yelled through the wall.

"I'm coming!" Everly called out, then opened her mouth wide with her eyebrows arched high and a silent laugh on her lips. "Get it? I'm coming?"

Surprised, Brighton huffed air in shocked snickering.

A beat of silence was followed by a single booming laugh from the other side of the wall.

Drew snorted from so far away it was barely audible. "Her jokes are funnier."

"Okay," Bruiser said, his voice fading as he walked away from the trailer, "but it wouldn't have been as funny if I didn't set it up, though. Right?"

"Leave them alone," Brooke called.

Brighton led Everly to the bathroom, then let the tap water warm before he ran a clean washrag under it.

"What are you doing?"

*Cleaning you.*

He'd done it before, minus the warm water. Hell, he enjoyed it. She always relaxed under his diligent affection afterward and was always so appreciative when he treated her well. He cleaned her carefully, then washed his hands. Not because he wanted to rinse her scent off his fingers and down the drain, but because he knew she'd be self-conscious if she thought the others could smell her on him. She tucked her towel back around her and followed him out.

The others were already headed for the rickety

old gate on the other side of the trailer park—the one that led to a worn trail up the mountain. The path they needed forked off that one. Most of the Ashe Crew was three sheets to the wind, shirtless and meandering into the woods barefoot, but Brooke, Skyler, and Danielle waited for them to catch up.

Brighton picked Everly up and jogged toward the receding group, determined to protect her flip-flop clad feet from the six inch weed garden they'd managed to grow in the back of the trailer yards over the summer. When he reached Brooke, he set Everly down and winked at his alpha's mate, then swatted his woman firmly on her perfect ass and trotted up the trail after the guys.

With one ear on the conversation around him and one on the conversation the girls were carrying on behind, he made himself give Everly space to talk to her new friends. These women had been through the wringer for their mates and had come out strong as steel. It took a special kind of woman to accept a life out here with a crew of growly, foul-mouthed, beer-guzzling, dirty-joking grizzly shifters. Everly would need to learn to depend on them when things got overwhelming or when she thought of questions pertinent to lady bears that he wouldn't have the answers to. He'd seen the bond between Brooke, Skyler, and Danielle and wished for that for Everly. She'd often talked about wanting friendship like that but had been unable to fit in anywhere in her old life.

From the way they were giggling and cutting up back there, his heart filled with the confidence that she was going to be okay here with him. With his people.

"Geez, brother," Denison said, hooking an arm around his neck. "You should see the sappy look on your face right now."

*I'm happy.*

Denison stopped so fast, Haydan ran into the back of him. Stumbling and slurring an oath, the other shifter walked around, but Denison just stared at Brighton like he hadn't understood the words he'd mouthed.

*I'm happy*, Brighton repeated.

A slow smile spread Denison's lips, then faded as he nodded. His brother ghosted a look behind him at Everly, then squeezed Brighton's upper arm and strode up the trail behind Tagan. Over his shoulder, he said, "Good. You deserve to be happy."

# THIRTEEN

"So many giant penises," Everly muttered.

"I know," Skyler said. Her dark hair swished around her bare shoulders as she shook her head in mock sadness. "They really have no shame, and I'm pretty sure modesty doesn't even exist here."

"She says as she sits spread-legged and naked on the river bank," Danielle ribbed, bumping Skyler's shoulder.

Brooke snorted and rubbed her belly. She wore a bright yellow bikini and leaned back on a locked arm, legs crossed in front of her.

"Can I feel?" Everly asked. Heat filled her cheeks

as she realized how inappropriate that must've sounded. "I'm so sorry. It's not... It's not my place to be rubbing all over your belly."

"I don't mind," Brook said. She snatched Everly's hand and placed her palm on one side. "I think this is his knee or elbow." A distracted look came over Brooke's face, and her belly jumped. "There. Did you feel it?"

How amazing that such a miracle existed. Against the odds, Brooke was carrying a cub, and without the heartache of years of trying, like Brighton had said most shifters had to go through. This child was truly meant to be a part of this place, and she'd felt him move, right against her palm. "That's like magic."

"Feels like it sometimes."

Most of the men were in the river, taking turns on a dangerous looking rope swing that dangled out from a branch across the gentle rapids. Apparently, they were trying to outdo each other with flips before they hit the water.

Drew yelled, "Watch out!" and jumped over the women's heads and into the water, laughing as they ducked.

"Dick," Danielle accused, but she was smiling so the insult lost its sting.

Everly liked the way they called names here. The words were jokes and terms of endearment, not spoken to hurt like Momma used to do.

"Brighton said it's hard for shifters to get pregnant," Everly said low.

"It is," Brook agreed. "We got lucky. Do you want a cub someday?"

Everly arced her gaze to Brighton as he swung out far over the water and jack-knifed with a big old grin on his face. He flipped Bruiser off right before he hit the water.

"I haven't really thought about it. I was raised in a different sort of home and thought I wouldn't ever want to raise a baby. I thought I wouldn't have the right tools to be a good momma, you know? But with Brighton, I think I would be okay. Some day. And it would be nice to bear him a cub. A baby who looks like him. If he wanted one, or course," Everly said, shaking her head self-consciously.

She petted the little pygmy goat that had followed Danielle out here and was now curled up in a comfortable-looking ball of gray fur next to her legs.

He had short curved horns that he attempted to use frequently on the boys, but with the women, he seemed to be a loyal, sweet little critter. Bo, Danielle had called him, bleated softly and nibbled at the edge of her towel.

"How do you handle being human around all this chaos?" she asked Danielle.

"I don't know," she answered, lifting her gaze from Bo to Denison. "I guess I love Denny so much that it doesn't matter that I'm different."

Thoughts of Connor and how forceful he'd been raised questions that sickened Everly's stomach. "Aren't you afraid of some other crew deciding to claim you since you don't bear Denison's mark?"

Danielle snorted and grinned. "This twatwaffle named Matt came on strong when I first arrived. He's a Gray Back. Brighton beat the shit out of him at the Lumberjack Wars competition for messing with me, and if he pushed anymore, I'm pretty sure Denison would've chopped him up into little cubes and pissed on the pile. Now, Matt and I have an understanding when I see him in town. He stays out of my way, and I don't sick the Ashe Crew on him. Look at them," she said, nodding her chin at the giant, eight-pack-riddled grizzly shifters in front of them. "Who in their right mind is going to take a mate away from one of them? It's a death sentence. I don't know. It just never felt right for me to change that much about myself to fit with Denison. We work as we are, different or not."

Everly liked that. She appreciated they were each different and had their own unique stories with their mates. She identified with the fact that none of their pairings had been easy. Now, she didn't feel alone with what Connor had done. It was just part of her tale that made her and Brighton unique, too.

The moon, low and heavy in the sky tonight, cast blue light across the woods. From here, she could make out the piney mountains on both sides of the river and the occasional fluffy cloud in the dark sky. A wide yellow moonbeam rippled across the water as the men stuck their splashy landings. The air was filled with the scent of sap and damp earth.

Denison came up the bank from the water, splashing around like the swamp thing. At least he had decided to wear swim trunks, unlike the others. Danielle squealed as he threw her over his shoulder and carried her into the waves. She gave a half-hearted struggle just before her new husband dunked her.

Brighton's turn was up again, and he stood on the opposite bank, bare torso stretched, muscles flexing as he held onto the rope above his head. He winked at Everly just before he backed up and launched himself into the water.

She giggled and leaned back on her elbows, feeling less and less bashful by the minute. She'd never seen Brighton like this—in his element and happy. It was good for her soul to see him completely at ease.

Brooke and Skyler watched Brighton as he crested the water and shook out his hair.

"Do his scars hurt you?" Brooke asked in a voice as soft as a breath.

Everly studied the stripes across her mate's smooth flesh as he dragged his feet and exited the water down the bank. "They did before I knew how he got them. Now, I adore them. They are one of the most attractive things about him because I know how strong my mate is. Those scars show his resilience."

"He told you how he got them?" Skyler asked, sitting up straighter.

Denison, who'd apparently heard the turn in

their conversation, drifted closer and settled Danielle against his chest.

"Yes. He told me."

"Told you?" Denison asked, cocking his head and frowning.

Brighton was walking toward them with a half-smile on his face, and Everly offered him a little wave. "Yes," she said. "He told me."

"You mean he wrote it down for you," Denison said, a statement, not a question.

The smile dropped from Brighton's face as he approached.

Confused at the change in the mood, Everly explained, "No, he *told* me."

Denison's dark eyebrows arched, and he dragged his gaze to Brighton. "What does she mean?"

Brighton linked his hands behind his head and stared at his brother with regret pooling in his eyes. He swallowed hard and winced. "I don't write my thoughts to her," Brighton whispered out in a painful-sounding hiss. "Not anymore."

Denison's eyebrows rose higher, and now he looked hurt. And angry. "What the fuck, man?" His voice wrenched up. "You can talk?"

Danielle dipped lower in the water behind Denison with her lips pursed and a troubled look on her face.

"Oh, shit," Everly said on a breath. "I didn't know—"

Denison shook his head hard, strode from the gently lapping water, and marched past Everly toward the trail.

Brighton looked sick as he followed his brother.

Heart in her throat, Everly stood and ran after them. She had to fix this somehow. She'd wanted his brother to like her, and instead, she'd made him feel alienated.

Up ahead, Denison was on his hands and knees in the dirt with Brighton crouched down beside him. Brighton made a calming gesture with his hands, and she halted a few feet away.

"Why didn't you tell me?" Denison asked in a choked voice. "Why didn't you ever talk to me?"

"Because it hurts to whisper," Brighton said, gripping the back of his brother's neck. "It feels like pushing glass shards up my throat. And more than that, it reminded me of when we were taken—of when Reynolds took my voice."

"You could've talked to me about that at any time, though, Brighton. I've always been here. I could see what it did to you, and you wouldn't ever open up or tell me what you remembered."

"Because, Denison, I was trying to protect you. You don't remember it all, but if I tell you all that happened, to me and what I saw them do to you, it'll bring it back. I know it will. I don't want that for you. You were lucky. You found peace. I couldn't rip that away from you."

Denison sat down hard and rested his elbows on his knees, then cupped his scalp in his oversize hands. His voice came out a tortured whisper, matching Brighton's. "I want to know everything. You shouldn't have gone through that alone. I can handle it. Knowing is better than imagining the worst."

Brighton's face crumpled, and he wiped the back of his hand across his eyes. "I'll tell you everything if that's what you want, but not here. Not on your wedding night. This can wait another day. It's held all this time."

Most of Denison's face was hidden, but Everly could see his lip tremble right before he said, "It's so fuckin' good to hear your voice again, Brigh."

Brighton pursed his lips as his eyes filled with sadness. "It's not really a voice, brother."

Denison sniffed and shook his head. "It's more than I ever thought I'd hear again."

Brighton cupped his brother's neck, then rested his head against his for a moment before he stood. Her mate scrubbed his hand down his face and tried to smile at her. It was a broken expression, though, and she reached for him. Held him tight. And when she looked up into his eyes again, she expected them to be silver, like they always seemed to be when he got too close to his secrets. To her unending relief, his eyes were still the color of spring grass.

Turning, she knelt down beside Denison. "I'm so sorry. I didn't know you hadn't heard him whisper. We were off in our own little world out at the cabin, and I didn't know the dynamics. I'm so sorry. Please forgive me."

"Forgive you?" Denison asked, a truly baffled expression on his face—a face so much like the man she loved. He shot up and took her with him, hugging her until she couldn't breathe. "There's nothing to forgive," he said thickly. "You brought my brother back. Thank you. Thank you," he choked out.

Twin tears streaked down her face as the big, burly shifter crushed her to him harder, then released her. Denison wiped moisture from his eyes and paced a short circle in front of her. "If you ever need anything," he said to her, "anything at all, you come to me and I'll take care of it. I owe you…" He shook his head as if his voice was going to fail. His expression was raw and open as he tried again. "I owe you everything."

Her throat clogged with emotion, and she nodded through her streaking tears. "Okay."

Denison squeezed her shoulder, then hugged his brother roughly with two resounding slaps on the back, then ducked around him and disappeared through the trees, headed back for the river.

"Brighton?" she asked, turning slowly toward her mate.

His chest heaved, scars stark, ribs showing and torso flexing with the movement. His hands were hooked on his hips, and he couldn't seem to meet her eyes quite yet.

"Can you take me home?"

His chin dipped slightly. He gripped her hand and led her back down the trail toward the trailer park.

He didn't say a word as they made their way back to his trailer. And when they were inside, she locked the door behind them and turned slowly. He watched her with a confused expression. *You okay?*

She swallowed and inhaled a slow breath. "Brighton, I don't want Connor's mark anymore. I want yours."

He shook his head slightly, and his look of profound confusion grew deeper, etching a wrinkle of worry across the bridge of his nose.

"What I mean to say is I want you to claim me."

Brighton's face went blank, and his ears moved slightly as the realization of what she was asking hit him. *I don't want to hurt you.*

"It'll be a temporary hurt that will bind me to you. I don't want to be Ashe Crew as a default member. I want to be Ashe Crew because I'm yours and I belong here. I want to be bound by your traditions. By *our* traditions," she amended. "I want to be proud of the scar on my back, not reminded of what Connor did to me." She lifted her chin and conjured her courage. "I want you to choose me."

"Done," he whispered without hesitation. His lips

crashed onto hers, and he plunged his tongue into her mouth. Gripping her hair, he angled her face as his lips moved against hers. Easing back slightly, he whispered, "I choose you."

Backing her toward the bedroom, he unsnapped her swimsuit top and pulled off her bikini bottom. His hands were everywhere, stroking, kneading, and adoring her skin. He dipped down, drew her nipple into his mouth, and sucked. His tongue stroked her until it was a hard bud, causing every nerve to tingle from there to her sex. He cupped his hand between her legs and pressed his finger into her, then smiled against her lips. His breath came in shallow bursts as he pressed his thick erection against her belly.

"Connor hurt you when he took you from behind because he did it wrong. I won't hurt you," he promised as he positioned her on the bed, hands and knees splayed.

"Angle your hips, love." He gripped her waist and guided her.

Fear and anticipation blasted through her like warring lightning strikes as the head of his cock touched her exposed slit. She gripped the soft comforter, preparing for the excruciating pain she knew was coming. But when he slid into her halfway, she didn't feel discomfort at all. Only a slight stretching and pleasure. He gave her another slow, shallow thrust, then pulled out again, teasing her.

Brighton pressed her fingertips between her legs, against the sensitive spot he always paid attention to, and she moaned and arched her back at the potent bliss the friction created.

"Touch here for me, baby," he whispered in a soft stroke against her ear.

His powerful hips moved against her backside as he thrust deeper into her.

"Holy fuck," he whispered in a shaky voice.

His chest rested against the curve of her back, from hips to shoulder blades, as if he couldn't get close enough to her skin. The slick sound of him sliding in and out of her was the sexiest thing she'd ever heard. His arm locked against the bed, beside hers, and his tricep flexed as he pressed into her again and again.

Unable to control herself, she was moaning now, louder with each stroke. "Brighton," she gasped out, so close to spilling over the edge. Breathily, she panted his name over and over as he grazed his teeth against the back of her neck.

She wanted it now, his bite. There was no fear, only desire to be bound to him. To be his mate in every way that counted. To banish Connor's ghost from the darkest corner of her life.

The humming sound she adored rattled from his middle as he clamped his teeth down on top of the scar Connor had made all those months ago. Brighton's cock swelled inside of her as he pushed into her faster. The stinging pain in her shoulder blade was overshadowed by the pleasure of her crashing orgasm. A deep growl rattled past her lips as Brighton froze and bit down into her muscle. Warmth spilled into her in hot, rhythmic jets as he came with her.

She cried out, bowing against his teeth as her gratification became blinding.

Her arms wouldn't hold her anymore, and she sank forward as he released her from his bite. Brighton gripped her waist and stroked into her slowly, drawing her aftershocks.

She let off a sigh of pure relief. This time had been totally different. The pain she remembered from intimacy with Connor didn't exist with Brighton. He loved her, adored and accepted her, where her first accidental mate had not.

Brighton's tongue was warm and soothing as he licked and kissed her new wound clean. He seemed in no hurry to withdraw from her, happy instead to take care of her injury. He didn't say the words here in the dark, but he didn't have to. His gentle affection showed his love and devotion to her.

Today, she'd become Ashe Crew and had discovered her place in the world. But more than that, she'd done something she never would've thought herself brave enough to do. She gave all of herself to her mate, and in return, he'd done the same for her.

Nothing could come between them now.

Connor's ghost held no place in her life anymore.

She belonged to Brighton, and he belonged to her.

# FOURTEEN

Bruiser's trailer banging commenced at approximately the ass-crack of dawn.

Everly had been snuggled up in Brighton's arms, but at the deafening noise, she jumped and yelped.

"Claws, woman," Brighton whispered. "Retract the claws."

She was digging into his skin hard enough to make perfect nail indentations.

"Oh, lovebears! It's initiation day," Bruiser called out in a sing-songy voice. "Wakey, wakey, I made you pancakeys."

"He's bribing you out of the trailer," Brighton

said in an amused rasp. "The boys made bets last night on what color your grizzly is. They've never met a submissive, so they're curious."

"My coloring has nothing to do with my submissiveness, though," she pointed out.

"No, but they'll use any excuse to make a bet."

"Who got closest?"

"Denison guessed blond. He'll never let anyone live it down after he figures out he got close enough."

She huffed a laugh and snuggled closer, inhaling the crisp scent of his skin. "I don't want to get out of bed today."

"I like the way that sounds." Brighton pulled her hand in a long stroke against his morning erection.

"Pancakes!" Bruiser yelled.

Brighton shook his head and narrowed his eyes at the ceiling, then kissed her forehead and rolled out of bed.

They dressed and readied for the day amid flirty touches and whispered endearments. Everything was different now. She wasn't some honorary member of the Ashe Crew anymore. She was in this, a part of life here, and claimed by the best man she'd ever known. Excitement bubbled inside of her at the thought of telling her new friends about the life-altering event that had happened last night.

Bruiser filled up the doorway with his humongous shoulders, blotting out the early morning light completely. His dark eyes danced as he held out a plate stacked high with buttered, syrup-soaked pancakes. "Chop, chop. Your new alpha is waiting." He moved to the side to reveal Tagan talking quietly to Brooke beside their trailer as he rubbed his hands over her round belly.

She and Brighton gobbled down a few flavorful griddlecakes, shoved the rest in the fridge, and bounded down the porch stairs after Bruiser. Brighton's claiming mark had covered Connor's scar and was still red and angry looking, but it didn't hurt much. The T-shirt she wore only irritated it a little. She predicted that in a day or so, she wouldn't feel it at all.

"Ready?" Tagan called.

Everly felt the urge to hunch into herself at the extra attention, but her need to answer the alpha won out. "As I'll ever be."

The Ashe Crew poured from the trailers, some tired and hungover, others happily greeting the others. She could easily weed out the morning people from the rest. Brooke waved and settled in beside her as the crew made their way to the gate they'd used last night. Skyler slung an arm around Everly's shoulders, and Danielle followed closely, reprimanding Bo for eating the page out of a sketch pad she was toting.

She was glad that even human, Danielle was a part of everything that went on here. Brighton had said she was some sort of environmentalist, studying the beetle infestation in the mountains for their boss. Her khakis, hiking boots, backpack, and constant note-taking and plant-collecting supported that.

At a clearing, Tagan pulled off his shirt and tossed it across a low-hanging limb of a giant tree. The other shifters followed suit, all but Brooke, who explained she hadn't had the urge to shift since she'd become pregnant. Probably best since Everly couldn't even begin to imagine the trauma of a Change on a little unborn baby.

Brighton couldn't seem to stop looking at her, and she got that. She was having trouble keeping her attention on where she put her hiking boots on the rugged trail. Her handsome mate's eyes were full of pride as he stood in front of her and carefully pulled the hem of her shirt over her head.

Leaning forward, he kissed her neck, bringing a shiver of pure pleasure up her spine. Then slowly, he turned her, so that her back was exposed to the Ashe Crew.

Brooke was the first one to her. "I knew it. I knew he'd claim you." She hugged Everly tight and turned to her mate. "Tagan, didn't I tell you he'd claim her?"

"You did," the alpha said as he gathered Everly into an embrace. "Congratulations, you two. I couldn't be happier for you."

The others followed, hugging, embracing, and slapping Brighton on the back as he grinned down at her. When Denison embraced his brother, he murmured something into his ear too low for Everly to hear.

"Hey there, sister," Danielle said in a choked voice as she squeezed her.

Everly's breath caught in her throat. She'd always wished for a sister, and it hadn't struck her until now that Brighton had given her even more than she'd realized.

She had a family now. Not one like she had with Momma, who was ruthless and used her love as a weapon. Everly had a real family, who fought and made up and loved each other unconditionally. She had people she would always be able to depend on. People who could depend on her.

"Come on out, beautiful bear," Brighton whispered. "It's time to meet your crew."

The last layer of reserve slipped from her shoulders as she undressed the rest of the way, then stood back and closed her eyes. Reaching deep within her, she conjured her bear. And as her animal burst forth, it hurt less this time, as if that part of her was meant to be here with her people.

"Holy mother of pearl," Drew breathed, gripping one of Tagan's shoulders and shaking the alpha slowly. "She's albino. Everly's a damned silver bear."

The wide-eyed Crew watched her as she settled to all fours. Head lowered, eyes downcast, she waited as Brighton Changed beside her.

Her mate was humming that happy noise as he nuzzled her face—her apparent reward for being brave and Changing for Ashe Crew to see.

Denison pointed to Haydan, Bruiser, and Drew

and crowed, "You all owe me money. I guessed blond."

The others Changed, one by one, and approached slowly. They pressed their noses against her fur, and she inhaled their scents in return until she recognized them all. Red bear, black bear, blond bear, gray bear. They all had human names. And last of all, Skyler's falcon erupted from her in a flurry of feathers. She flapped her powerful wings as she beat air currents that lifted her into the sky.

Tagan bellowed out three short roars and twitched his head. Danielle and Brook flanked him as he meandered into the trees, and the bears followed behind as Skyler circled above.

Brighton stepped in front of Everly and looked back over his shoulder, as if he was unsure if she would follow.

He needn't worry. She'd always be here, right beside him, quietly ghosting the edges of the Ashe Crew with the man she loved. With the man whose soft whisper had resonated so loudly in the course of her life.

Everly would follow him always.

# EPILOGUE

Brighton listened to the long note and twisted one of the tuning pegs on his guitar until it sounded just right. Sammy's bar was full of shifters tonight, though the bartender didn't have a clue his joint was overrun with supernaturals. Tagan had decided more communication with the Gray Backs and Boarlanders would benefit all three crews, so once a month they drank booze together, shot pool, talked shop, and got to know each other on a friendly level.

Jed, the last alpha, would've never sanctioned relationships between the rival crews like this, but that's what made Tagan a good leader. He looked to the future.

Denison gave him a *here-we-go* look and Brighton nodded out a three count, then strummed the first chord to the next song in the set. Denison's voice came out steady and strong through the microphone as he played his guitar along with Brighton. The lights weren't as bright on the stage tonight, and thank God for small blessings, because from here, Brighton had the perfect view of his mate.

Everly sat at the bar next to her Momma. Brighton had watched a change in Everly from the time he'd found her in the diner until now. She'd realized how unhealthy the relationship with her mom was and put her foot down. Her Momma clung to the habit of insulting her from time to time, and Everly had left the situation immediately. The bitter name-calling had tapered off as the woman seemed to be learning that behavior was unacceptable. If she wanted a relationship with Everly, or with him, or with any future grandkids they might give her, then Momma Moore had to learn how to be a kind and respectful person around them.

The silver-haired woman took another pull of her beer and laughed at something Everly said.

Brighton smiled and dragged his attention to the fret of his guitar as he hit a harder chord.

Her relationship with her mother wasn't the only thing that had changed. Everly was now a working member of the Ashe Crew, and they were close to paying off her medical bills from when she'd had the seizures. She'd paid back her landlord her late rent and broke the lease early. And since logging season had begun a few months ago, she had been driving truckloads and trailers of stripped lumber to the sawmill in Saratoga or to meet with the log buyers. She was even getting good at haggling prices, thanks to Tagan taking the time to train her properly. Submissive or not, she was smart as a whip and had the backbone to go along with it now.

He was so damned proud of her, he couldn't quit grinning. Denison and the guys ribbed him constantly for it, but they didn't know how dark things had really been. And because of that, they didn't understand just how much Everly had done for him to get him to a place where he was this happy. Denison had once said he owed her everything for bringing Brighton back to him. Well, Brighton owed her everything as well.

Denison sang the last line of the song, and the bar erupted in cheers. Brighton stood up to the microphone and waited for the ruckus to settle. He wasn't afraid of his whisper anymore. Not when Everly loved it so much. He was proud of it. If this was the only sound he had left after what he'd been through, well hell, at least it was something. At least he was still breathing, kicking, fighting, and trying after what Reynolds did. Better than that sonofabitch lying cold in a shallow grave somewhere.

Brighton blew an ear-splitting whistle, and the bar settled, grew quiet. "Denison and I have special guest singers tonight, and I want you all to give them a real warm welcome. It's their first time on stage ever, and you get to be a part of it. Skyler Brown and Everly Moore, soon to be Everly Beck, come on up here."

Everly gave Skyler an excited grin as her Momma looked at her with utter shock written across her face. Everly picked up two shot glasses of what looked like whiskey, then weaved her way through the tables in front of Skyler. Someday, he was going to get his mate up here with that pretty voice of hers and just him on the guitar, but for now, she said she'd only do this if Skyler, Kellen's little songbird, sang a duet with her. And as Brighton watched the easy smile that graced his woman's lips, he thought it was the right decision. She didn't even look scared. She looked strong and sexy as hell in those tight jeans and black tank top.

Confidence sure did look good on her.

As they approached the stage to the cheers and whistles of the crews, Everly handed Skyler one of the shots, and they clinked the tiny glasses, then downed the fragrant liquid. Everly took Brighton's offered hand and stepped up on stage, then pushed his chest until he sat in the chair. She bent forward and kissed him, releasing half the fiery shot into his mouth in what had to be the sexiest toast he'd ever been a part of. He smiled against her lips and swallowed it down. To the whistles of the bar, he pressed his tongue against the closed seam of her lips until she let him in. She giggled as she pecked him once more and pulled away, then leaned back in, grabbed his shirt, and whispered, "I sure do love you, Brighton Beck."

"I love you, too, Everly Beck."

She flashed the thin gold band lined with tiny

diamonds on her ring finger and shook her head with a wink. "Soon to be."

Pleased, he dipped his head to hide the heat that crept into his cheeks and the grin that took his face. Damn, that woman could get his pulse racing.

She bumped Skyler's shoulder, then took a deep breath and nodded to him and Denison. Brighton tapped out a three count with the toe of his boot, and he and his brother picked up the first notes of the song.

Everly's voice came clear and low, and Skyler joined in at a higher harmony. They patted the legs of their jeans and shimmied along to the lyrics like they'd done this on stage a thousand times. Their voices were perfectly harmonized, and Denison shot him an impressed look before he dragged his gaze back to Danielle, who sat at her favorite table in the front row.

The bar was still, other than the occasional whistle and "Yeah!" from the onlookers.

Tagan had his arm around Brooke, who would bear him a cub any day now. A baby for the Ashe Crew, who would grow up knowing his place in the world, surrounded by a giant, grizzly-shifting, fun-loving family who'd do anything to keep him safe.

Drew, Haydan, and Bruiser were taking shots at the bar, while Kellen sat by Danielle, watching Skyler as if he'd never seen anyone so beautiful. Brighton knew that feeling. He felt the same about Everly.

Intermingled in the crowd were the other crews, determined to forge friendships to preserve their way of life. If there was safety in numbers, well, Saratoga was just about the safest place a bear shifter could be now.

Brighton strummed alongside his brother and watched Everly's profile as she closed her eyes and belted out the chorus into the microphone as if she'd been born to sing on stage. She didn't normally like the attention, he knew that, but a few months ago, she would've panicked just thinking about doing something like this. Now here she was, grinning at Skyler like she was having the time of her life and shooting him happy looks over her shoulder at the breaks in the song.

She was so damned beautiful he couldn't look away if he tried.

Everly didn't know what she'd done for him, and he could never explain the depth of his gratitude for the changes she'd started in him. She'd vanquished his ghosts and offered him peace.

Swearing off a mate hadn't worked. Not when she hadn't cared about how damaged he'd been. She'd seen his potential and encouraged him to quit hiding. His small-town, shy, unknowingly beautiful girl had come in and turned his world upside down.

And now Ever, forever and ever, would be the keeper of his heart.

## SAWMAN WEREBEAR

## Want More of the Saw Bears?

The Complete Series is Available Now

Other books in this series:

### Lumberjack Werebear
(Saw Bears, Book 1)

### Woodcutter Werebear
(Saw Bears, Book 2)

### Timberman Werebear
(Saw Bears, Book 3)

### Axman Werebear
(Saw Bears, Book 5)

### Woodsman Werebear
(Saw Bears, Book 6)

### Lumberman Werebear
(Saw Bears, Book 7)

## About the Author

T.S. Joyce is devoted to bringing hot shifter romances to readers. Hungry alpha males are her calling card, and the wilder the men, the more she'll make them pour their hearts out. She werebear swears there'll be no swooning heroines in her books. It takes tough-as-nails women to handle her shifters.

Experienced at handling an alpha male of her own, she lives in a tiny town, outside of a tiny city, and devotes her life to writing big stories. Foodie, wolf whisperer, ninja, thief of tiny bottles of awesome smelling hotel shampoo, nap connoisseur, movie fanatic, and zombie slayer, and most of this bio is true.

Bear Shifters? Check

Smoldering Alpha Hotness? Double Check

Sexy Scenes? Fasten up your girdles, ladies and gents, it's gonna to be a wild ride.

For more information on T. S. Joyce's work,
visit her website at
www.tsjoyce.com

Made in the USA
Coppell, TX
17 April 2023

15708297R00132